When his
darkness h
consciousn
there passi
had happened to him or all would be lost. With sudden inspiration he put out his tongue and found himself licking plastic. A thrill of terror swamped his mind for a moment. Suddenly things were falling into place. Pictures flashed through his mind, crystallising the terrible knowledge of what had happened.

A sob tore from his throat with the realisation that, trapped in a body bag, he lay among plague victims awaiting cremation.

Also by Mark Ronson
in Hamlyn Paperbacks

BLOODTHIRST
GHOUL
OGRE

PLAGUE PIT

Mark Ronson

Hamlyn Paperbacks

For Captain Tico

This is a fictional story
set in the near future –
only the plague pits are real.

PLAGUE PIT
ISBN 0 600 20230 5

First published in Great Britain 1981
by Hamlyn Paperbacks

Hamlyn Paperbacks are published by
The Hamlyn Publishing Group Ltd,
Astronaut House,
Feltham,
Middlesex, England

(Paperback Division: Hamlyn Paperbacks,
Banda House, Cambridge Grove,
Hammersmith, London W6 0LE)

Printed and bound in Great Britain by
Cox & Wyman Ltd, Reading

PROLOGUE

Hi London, this is Phil Jason with an early morning warning that it's a miserable day – near freezing outside – so why not pamper yourselves with a few extra minutes in bed with the friendly sound of Radio City. Beep! Beep! Yes, I've got the klaxon repaired. I also have to report that alone of mankind I've eluded the cold bug. Beep! Talking of germs, in News-flash *I'll bring you the latest on those East German germs, also what the new Prime Minister says about four million unemployed. Beep! But if you're depressed with the world and the weather there's still a silver lining – tonight is* Charity Show *night. Now, let's spin off with the latest from The Strippers . . .*

Hacker jabbed the 'off' button of the bedside radio, cursed the December bleakness pervading the flat and focussed his gaze on the serene face with its halo of soft curls on the pillow beside him. How innocent Audrey looked asleep – hard to imagine that she was a whore. When a phone call threw her into a frenzy of dressing before the arrival of a minicab, she explained she was wanted as a stand-in night-club hostess, a euphemism which neither took seriously.

He knew that if he touched her – it had been one of her working nights – she would mutter something incomprehensible and turn away, so Hacker pulled on his work clothes and switched on the electric kettle in the cramped kitchenette. The gall in his mouth was not only from last night's lonely debauch – there was something about his present life poisoning him.

'Now is the winter of our discontent . . . '

The words, stored in subconscious memory since college days, could not have been more apt. Life had become a sham. In trendy pubs and on building sites he boasted that he'd dropped out of university in disgust at the bourgeois system – in reality he had not been capable of staying the course.

Now, shaving above the cluttered sink, Hacker saw that he was as phoney as Audrey who was always talking about a future stage career. He knew he must escape this dead end, this rathole of a flat, his dreary workmates and a wife who came home with the stink of strangers upon her.

This time, he told himself, he would break free. Through dirty glass he gazed at the grieving angels of Fulham cemetery, but in his mind's eye he saw an endless expanse of sea.

'Hacker!'

The foreman's harsh voice sliced the curtain of drizzle shrouding the City building site. In a corrugated iron shelter the small workforce, in yellow PVC jackets and construction helmets, looked up from their poker game to Hacker's JCB. It was shovelling up the rubble of ancient buildings to make way for an Arab bank whose dark-glassed tower was planned to be the tallest in London.

After more shouts, and delighted gestures from the poker players, Hacker became aware of Mr Jennings framed in the doorway of his caravan office. He slewed his vehicle and gunned it across the clay with its saw-toothed scoop lowered as though to sweep away both foreman and caravan. At the last moment he braked and raised the scoop on its hydraulic arm rather as a well-trained elephant would salute a rajah. The effect was not lost on the spectators.

'Sure now, he's got that creetur eating out of his hand,' a weathered Dubliner exclaimed in mock admiration.

'Ferris, you're drunk again,' snapped the foreman.

'No sorr, never,' protested Michael Ferris, slipping into his role of stage Irishman. 'Not a dhrop has passed me lips. To be sure, the holy hour lasts all day for me, your honour.' His horny hand closed over a flat pint bottle in the hip pocket of his dungarees.

Hacker tipped the scoop so that clods scattered wildly

and killed the engine.

'Yes, Mr Jennings,' he said in a deceptively respectful tone. His shoulder-length hair, held by a tennis player's headband, and his wolfish features gave him a rebellious air which made his mates wary of him although his antics frequently relieved the tedium of work.

'Are you a bleeding idiot, Hacker?' demanded the foreman.

In his cab Hacker considered the question, then asked deferentially, 'Have I done something wrong again, Mr Jennings?'

Leroy Delgardo, who still had West Indian sunshine in his soul, was so overcome by Hacker's dead pan humour that he emitted a piercing giggle.

'Shut up, Midnight, or he'll have us both deported,' Ferris hissed in pretended terror.

'You there,' Jennings shouted. 'The rain's cleared so what the hell are you hanging round for? Start shifting them pipes in the far corner.'

Reluctant to miss the fun, the men moved slowly.

'Now listen to me, Hacker,' the foreman resumed. 'You may think you're smart to have dropped out of college and come slumming on building sites, but get it into your bleeding skull that here you have to do as you're told. How many times have I warned you to bleeding-well avoid that old brickwork? If I hadn't yelled out you'd have been into it, and there would've been hell to pay . . . the GLC site inspector's been snooping around about it twice already. Either you stop poncing about like some Chelsea git or you collect your cards. And any more smart answers and we'll settle it man-to-man, if you get my meaning.'

Hacker nodded.

'Be careful of the old brickwork and keep a due sense of respect,' he said.

Jennings glowered at him but the situation was saved by the trilling of a telephone in the caravan. Hacker revved the engine to give the foreman the benefit of its roar, his contempt for Jennings only being matched by Jennings' dislike of him.

A minute later the caravan door slammed and the foreman yelled across the site, 'I've got to go to head office so keep at it. Henry, you're in charge and don't let that clown in the JCB near the brickwork.'

'Right, Mr Jennings,' said Henry Wilcox, savouring his brief promotion.

With the foreman's departure the men straightened up and lit cigarettes. On reaching the end of a row of T-shaped pegs, Hacker left the JCB idling and strolled across to cadge one.

'Maan, I sure laugh when you look at the boss that way,' Leroy Delgardo chuckled. 'Wonder why that old brick-work so damn important?'

'Perhaps it's some sort of boundary,' said a tow-haired youth in a studded motorcycle jacket.

'Huddy, any fool can see the boundary's further back,' declared Henry Wilcox.

They'll be open I'm thinking,' Ferris said. 'England expects, eh boys?'

Wilcox regarded his watch like a mariner checking a compass, then said, 'Right, men, lunch break.'

Reddened hands in pockets, shoulders hunched against the cold, the site-clearing gang straggled down a narrow street to the Lord Nelson. In its old-fashioned bar, with crimson wallpaper and steamy mirrors advertising Edwardian drinks, they ordered beer and meat pies, except Hacker who had a vodka and then decided he could use several more. His discontent was still gnawing him, aggravated by Jennings. Although he usually came off best in their verbal exchanges, the fact remained that the fore-man had the last laugh because he represented authority. It was there in his barrel-like body and his ham-like fist.

While he sulked over his vodka the others chatted with Hazel, the landlady, who turned an appropriate blind eye to their mud-caked boots. With beer costing over a pound a pint, she was grateful for their custom. While serving their second round she turned away to sneeze into a Kleenex.

'Oh dear,' she said. 'I do hope I haven't got that wretched super 'flu. Half my regulars are away with it. And no wonder when they go from the cold into hot, sticky Underground trains. Ideal breeding grounds for germs . . .'

'Huddy here knows all about germs,' said the sixth member of the group, an East Ender named Bob Blake. 'He comes from a place in Derbyshire where the whole village got the plague, don't you, son?'

Tom Hudson grinned foolishly.

'Never been right there since, have they, son?'

'It was a long time ago,' the youth explained, and was surprised when everyone guffawed.

'I should hope so, too,' said Hazel.

Returning to the site they found that the foreman was still absent.

'Mind how you go,' Wilcox told Hacker as he climbed into the JCB cab. 'Don't forget what Mr Jennings told you.'

'Stuff Jennings,' retorted Hacker, the alcohol in his blood magnifying the waves of protest sweeping him. He lowered the scoop and left a trail of diesel fume across the site.

'Look at Hacker,' cried Blake. ''E's flipped.'

The JCB snapped its way through a line of surveyors' pegs and the scoop smashed on to the forbidden brickwork.

'That'll show the bastard,' exulted Hacker. He swung the arm of the JCB and more ancient bricks and mortar exploded under the impact of the scoop.

'Stop him, men,' Wilcox shouted. 'Or Jennings'll cancel our bonuses.'

A whole section of brick paving collapsed inwards, leaving a jagged-gap from which rushed a gust of air so foul that the men nearby began to choke and retch.

'Bloody hell!' muttered Blake, backing away. 'The stupid berk's bust a sewer.'

Laughing at the screwed-up faces of his mates, Hacker swung himself out of the cab, then he too retreated as fetid air filled his nostrils.

'I feel better for that,' he boasted as he joined the group of hawking labourers. 'Only wish Jennings had been here to watch.'

'It may give you a laugh, but you've just sodding well lost us our bonuses,' shouted Wilcox, angry blood suffusing his fat features.

'I sure needed that bonus for Christmas,' Leroy

Delgardo said sadly. 'I promised my woman a music centre.'

'You piss me off,' Hacker snarled. 'It's only some old cellar full of stale air. I'll soon fill it in.'

He strode towards the scattered heaps of broken brick.

'The stink's gone already,' he shouted over his shoulder. 'That proves it wasn't a sewer . . . ' His voice trailed away as he gazed downwards.

'What is it?' called Ferris.

When Hacker made no reply the Irishman's curiosity drew him to the sagging lip of the cavity.

'Holy Saints preserve us,' he whispered. The others edged forward, their eyes following his trembling finger. Leering at them from the blackness of the pit was a human skull.

'An old burial ground,' said Wilcox. 'No wonder Jennings didn't want that brickwork touched.'

'Cover it up, 'tis a terrible thing to disturb the dead,' muttered Ferris, making a sign of the Cross.

'Hold on,' said Hacker. 'We may as well take a look. In Victorian times they used to bury them with their jewellery. Get a lantern, Huddy.'

The youth raced to the tool hut and returned with a battery lamp already switched on in his eagerness. As its beam probed the space beneath the brick paving, the men kneeling round the opening gasped in awe. Skeletal arms rose from mould as though petrified in the act of waving; skulls assumed eerie expressions as shadows danced in their eye sockets and half-buried rib cages gleamed like strange jetsam cast up on a dark shore.

Only Ferris spoke as the finger of light traversed the bone-littered space.

''Tis a potter's field,' he said. 'A place for those poor souls whose folk couldn't afford them decent burial.'

Something glinted.

Hacker snatched the lamp and lowered himself through the breach, carelessly pushing bones out of his way, and crawled towards the spark. His silent mates saw him tug at something attached to the neck of a skeleton. Vertebrae rolled in all directions but when he returned to the daylight he was swinging a chain with a small triangle attached to it.

'Gold!' hissed several voices.

Hudson reached forward and turned the metal, pointing to a curious arrangement of letters inscribed upon it.

ABRACADABRA
ABRACADABR
ABRACADAB
ABRACADA
ABRACAD
ABRACA
ABRAC
ABRA
ABR
AB
A

'Know what this is?' he demanded.

'Several hundred quids' worth,' grinned Blake.

'It's a plague charm.'

'If it was it didn't do the poor sod much good,' said Hacker. 'Anyway, how do you know?'

'At school we did the plague in a local history project,' the youth answered earnestly. 'In the Great Plague people wore these things for protection. Don't you see, this is a plague pit. They dug down to the water level and then buried them in layers from the carts of dead. This is the top layer after the soil has subsided. And that's why it was bricked over ages ago.'

'Hacker, you fill in that hole bloody quick,' Wilcox shouted. 'Them bones may be infected.'

'You crazy, Henry? The Plague of London was three centuries ago,' Hacker said derisively. 'There'll be more of these trinkets in there. I'm going back.'

He lowered himself into the space between the bone-littered soil and the blackened brick roof.

'Guess we shouldn't be doin' this,' muttered Leroy Delgardo, but like the others he seized a spade and followed Hacker into the pit.

Hudson dived forward. He had seen a brief gleam and

now his fingers closed on a small crucifix in which were embedded several cloudy-looking gems.

'Look, look,' he breathed, showing it to his mates whose eyes narrowed with treasure fever. Crouching low, or even crawling on their hands and knees, they spread out with their shadows performing a *danse macabre* around them. Boots snapped brittle bones and smashed skulls. As chalky powder rose from the remains they coughed and held handkerchiefs to their faces.

Leroy Delgardo pointed to something reflecting the glow of his lighter from within a framework of rib bones. Hacker swung his beam on to the spot and a pile of discs was transmuted into gold. The Jamaican dropped his handkerchief and began to scrape away the detritus beneath the bones.

'Easy on, let it settle,' said Hacker, spitting in disgust. Glancing up at his mates even he was surprised by their faces. From expressions of good-natured apathy, they had become feral.

'He must have been chucked in with a bag of money under his clothes,' he said as the coins brightened with the thinning of the vapour-like dust. 'Those black ones could be silver.'

'Let's get out and divi up,' Ferris said. 'If there's anything else it'll be down below, and it's bad luck to dig up the dead.'

They climbed out, blinking in the dying light of the winter afternoon, and trooped to the shelter where the hoard was laid out on a copy of the *Sun*.

'We must keep quiet about this, men,' Wilcox declared. 'It's treasure trove and if the police get wind of it they'll confiscate the lot and we might be nicked for not handing it over.'

'Or for breaking into a plague pit,' muttered Hudson.

'Right, say nothing and we'll be rich,' Hacker said. 'Look at this piece, a Charles I noble. At today's gold price it's worth a fortune – and probably an even bigger one to a collector.'

'Let's share it then,' said Blake practically. 'We'll divide the stuff into six piles as equal as possible and then draw for them. Fair?'

The others nodded, all except Hudson.

'I want the cross.'

Hacker held it up to the light.

'Those stones are only moonstones,' he said. 'You can keep it and we'll share the coins.'

A shadow fell across them. At the door stood the foreman, his face a dangerous crimson and his eyes bulging with anger.

'I had a little accident, Mr Jennings,' Hacker said calmly. 'But we found something inside. Here's your share.'

He pressed several heavy coins into his hand. 'There's quite a few hundred nicker there. All right, Mr Jennings?'

For a long moment the foreman regarded the dull gold, then abruptly slipped it into his waistcoat pocket.

'The rain's coming back, so we'll call it a day,' he said. 'Before you go, Hacker, I want that hole in the brickwork filled. Pile mud over it natural-like, and let's hope the site inspector don't notice. In a few days it'll be concreted over.'

'Yes sir, Mr Jennings, two bags full,' muttered Hacker as he climbed into his cab and lowered the scoop. 'And up yours, Mr Jennings. This is the last you'll be seeing of me.'

That night the wife of Leroy Delgardo could hardly believe her ears when he said, 'Reckon it's time we took a holiday in Kingston to show those back-home folks how well we done in this town.'

At the same time Tom Hudson rode his Suzuki 250 over a wetly shining road which led to a teenage party, grinning to himself as the cool metal of the cross touched his skin.

In his Streatham semi-detached Henry Wilcox slumped with his wife in front of a TV comedy about a middle-aged couple in a semi-detached in Streatham. For once the conditioned reflex which prompted him to laugh in sympathy with electronic applause found no response – his mind was occupied with the amazing knowledge that he could pay off the mortgage which had been a millstone round his neck.

'Trouble is they ain't hall-marked,' hissed the dwarf in the back room of his jeweller's shop in East Ham.

'Okay, I'll try the British Museum.'

'Now Blakie, don't be hasty. Gimme another look.'

A few minutes later Blake went whistling into the night with a comforting wad in his breast pocket.

Michael Ferris left the Mother Redcap and reeled in the direction of a green light indicating a minicab office. Suddenly he felt an arm slide under his jaw and wrench his head back. In front of him a shadow materialised from a shadowed doorway, a fist thudded into his belly and a steel-capped boot caught him scientifically in the groin. The arm round his neck relaxed and he dropped to his knees, his outraged body regurgitating its sour cargo while expert hands frisked his pockets. As the footfalls of the muggers faded, a low moaning came from the victim's lips.

''Tis a judgement . . . a judgement . . . '

Hacker entered his flat and, after stowing a small packet at the back of a drawer, undressed and slid under the duvet next to Audrey.

'One for the road,' he muttered as his hand reached for her.

'What did you say?' she asked, her eyes widening into wakefulness. 'Oh, darling, you have caught a cold.'

1

. . . and this is Phil Jason bringing you Newsflash. *Despite firm denials by the Communist authorities, speculation rages regarding deaths said to be due to an accident in an East German bacteriological warfare laboratory. Unofficial reports reaching the West claim that the town of Volkstadt has been isolated following the decimation of its population by a mysterious viral epidemic. Fears have been expressed that the infection may have spread beyond the quarantined area, and in West Germany special medical teams are on standby.*

In a Camden Town back street Dr Aziz slowed his old Metro as he reached a row of once fashionable houses. Now their paint peeled. Graffiti – mostly referring to Ulster – disfigured their stonework while winter winds piled litter behind railings corroded by generations of dogs. Aziz sighed at the bleakness of the scene, its only hint of colour coming from a tattered election poster and a plastic Christmas tree behind a ground-floor window. He braked when he was abreast of a green door on which the number 103 appeared in a darker shade of paint, the shadows of old brass numerals which only recently had become worth stealing.

The doctor turned up his collar against the freezing morning and stepped carefully on the snow powdering the pavement. He pressed the bellpush several times and resigned himself to a long wait. After a couple of minutes the door opened suspiciously and a white-haired woman with swollen legs raked him with piercing blue eyes.

'Sorry, you'll have to try somewhere else,' she announced. 'All my rooms are let . . . oh, you're not the doctor, are you?'

By way of confirmation Aziz held up his black bag.

'I got such a turn when I seen him,' she said as he entered a dim vestibule. ''E was off work for a couple of days after he was mugged, quite poorly he was but not that bad if you get my meaning . . . I mean, there didn't seem to be anything wrong enough for him to turn black. His room is on the right on the top floor. Go on up, but I'll stay down here because of me legs.'

Aziz winced when he opened the door and approached the corpse. Michael Ferris lay on his back, his mouth open as though death had come in the middle of a shout. The doctor raised the blind and saw the skin was discoloured as if it was one vast bruise. Taking surgical gloves from his case, Aziz rolled back the blankets and deftly unbuttoned an old fashioned flannel vest. Seconds later he rushed from the room and turned the key behind him.

'What did it, doctor?' asked the landlady, waddling into the hallway. 'When will they take 'im away? While that room ain't let I'm losing money.'

'Madam, don't let a single soul near that room. Where can I telephone from?'

'There's a phone box round the corner. You can try that – if it ain't vandalised.'

Outside Dr Aziz was in such a hurry that he forgot his car and ran down the street.

'Health Department, duty officer speaking,' said the young man in the bright Civic Centre office. 'I see . . . what's your name, doctor?' He pulled a pad over to him. 'Name of the deceased and location . . . cause of death . . . what? Can you be sure?'

'I am telling you, man, in Calcutta I have seen . . . ' came the faint voice.

'All right, Dr Aziz. Let me jot down the symptoms . . . Can you speak more slowly please . . . N-E-C-R-O-T-I-C, yes, I've got that.'

He continued to write busily for a minute, then said, 'Stay with the deceased, will you, please, doctor. I must inform the Environmental Health Officer and the Proper

Officer who, if necessary, will alert the surrounding districts. We'll get a fumigation team over to you as fast as we can. Yes, if it's what you think the Health Officer may come personally, probably with a consultant . . . Yes, yes. Goodbye.'

The young man looked at the Yucca plant on the window sill and exhaled an exaggerated breath, then stabbed a number on his telephone.

'Betty, can I speak to himself . . . oh, sir, I've just had a call from a GP . . . '

He had to concentrate on keeping his voice steady.

'I agree it does sound far-fetched, sir,' he concluded. 'Yes, he is an Asian. But I don't think his lot drink, sir.'

The harsh protest of rooks filled the ancient burial ground. Amid the graves the plump clergyman watched the girl in the white trenchcoat adjust her Uher tape recorder.

'I am Charity Brown and today I am standing in St Lawrence's churchyard in the Derbyshire village of Eyam,' she told the slim microphone. 'In my search for forgotten heroines I am speaking to you from beside the grave of Catherine Mompesson . . . '

Switching off, Charity surveyed the ill-omened birds circling leafless trees. The vicar was suddenly conscious of her lustrous eyes which brought a necessary hint of mischief to a face of almost classic beauty.

'Sorry about the raucous wildlife,' he said. 'Would you rather make your recording in the church?'

She shook her head.

'If I explain what the noise is, it'll give some local colour.'

She raised the mike and continued in her husky professional voice: 'The rooks which are wheeling above me seem to be saying "Go! Go! Go!" – and their advice must have sounded like a sad mockery to the villagers when this lonely place became known as "The Plague Village" three centuries ago . . . '

Charity paused to glance at a clipboard balanced on a mossy tomb, then continued: 'Near to where I am standing there is an inscribed stone which reads: "Of the pestilence of 1666, at Eyam, 259 persons of ripe age and 58 children died out of a population of 350 souls." '

'This story goes back to a bleak September morning in 1665 when a cart pulled up outside the gate of George Vickers, the village tailor. He ran out to collect a special bolt of cloth he'd ordered from London, unaware that germs of bubonic plague were in its silken folds. He carried it inside and was soon busy turning it into a wedding dress for a local girl. When he snuffed out the candle late that night his head was throbbing.

'I worked too hard on that gown,' he told himself. But next day he was fighting for air. The dress was never finished and the young bride was destined never to walk up the church aisle for her marriage ceremony. Before long the unfortunate Vickers died. A purple blotch was found on his chest, the mark of the plague which had already killed thousands of Londoners 160 miles away. From one rose-covered cottage to another the germs spread and before the month was out, six people had died, each with the dreaded purple patch.

'Eyam was stunned. Who would be next to wake in a sick sweat? Panic built up until someone shouted the fatal words "Flee for your lives!" '

'Toys, household treasures and food were made into bundles as though an invading army were approaching. The villagers were ready to stampede when the young vicar, William Mompesson, begged them to consider what they were about to do.

'Unwillingly at first, they listened to him while he implored them not to spread the infection to nearby towns.

'My wife Catherine and I will stay with you,' he promised. 'Let us face this dreadful thing together.'

'His words made the villagers realise their duty to their fellow men and quietly they began to unpack their belongings, and wait – and die! The Reverend Mompesson listed their deaths in a Plague Register, and what everyday heroism is to be read between its fading lines!'

Pausing at intervals to check her notes, Charity went on to describe how, under the vicar's leadership, the village organised itself as though it were under siege. Hurdles were placed across roads to prevent strangers wandering into the danger zone, and a stone trough was set up marking the boundary between Eyam and the rest of the world. The villagers, too proud to accept charity even in their hour of need, filled it with vinegar as a primitive disinfectant and placed coins in it. Outsiders left food by the trough, scooped up the money in payment and ran. Today this trough has a spring bubbling out of it and it is known as Mompesson's Well.

Another of the rector's ideas was to abandon church services, as he feared infection would spread if his flock gathered in close contact. Instead, he held services in a tiny valley called Cucklet Dell, preaching in front of a natural arch of rock which echoed his words across a brook to the opposite slope where family groups stood apart from each other.

'As the weeks went by Eyam became a ghost village,' Charity continued. 'Grass sprouted between cobblestones, cows wandered the empty streets unmilked and the dead outnumbered the living. During one week an entire family died on a farm just outside Eyam. From a safe distance neighbours watched the mother, Mrs Hancock, dig a shallow grave and then drag out the body of her husband, followed by the bodies of her children. After that she was not seen again.

'One evening William Mompesson and Catherine walked in this churchyard and watched the sunset. Both were exhausted by nursing the sick and ministering to the dying.

'Catherine took her husband's hand, drew a deep breath and said, "How sweet smells the air." William's blood ran cold. An odd symptom of the plague was that when a victim was first infected he or she had the illusion of a pleasant scent in the nostrils. His wife's remark warned him that her death was close, and not long afterwards he added her name to the list of plague victims.

'After fourteen months the Eyam plague came to an end and outsiders ventured into the village to inquire about relatives, usually only to find their graves. But thanks to the inspiration of William and Catherine Mompesson, the dreadful infection did not spread to the surrounding countryside. William – to his surprise – had survived and he remained in Eyam for a further three years restoring life to the village of death.

'As I stand here by the grave of his wife I can only feel gratitude that modern medicine has freed us from the threat of such visitations . . .'

Charity snapped the mike switch and smiled at the clergyman.

'Would you have stayed?' she asked.

'I thank God that I am unlikely to be put to the test like my predecessor,' he answered. 'I must say that I envy you your fluency, Miss Brown. But, now, if you'll excuse me, I have a confirmation class . . . '

Thanking him, Charity put the carrying strap of the Uher over her shoulder and walked towards the church. As he watched her retreating figure, the vicar was struck by her unusually graceful gait. He imagined that in Biblical times the women who went to the well of Midian must have walked like that. Another thought came: How could people be racially intolerant when God had created such people as Charity black?

Inside the church Charity unslung her tape recorder and sat in a corner pew. From outside the cries of the rooks came but faintly, and she began to savour the tranquillity of the old building. Perhaps it was her family's tradition of church-going which made her responsive to churches despite the fact that her formal religious beliefs had been discarded when she became convinced she had lived previous lives and embraced the concept of reincarnation.

Tranquillity was something that Charity needed. During her recording her voice had not betrayed her underlying feelings but now the work was complete she allowed her mind to dwell sadly on a letter in her pocket. Early that morning she had picked it up from the Radio City office in Ludgate Circus, and she was still upset by its contents.

It had been sent to her by Paul Mitchell, a microbiologist she had interviewed a few weeks ago. The interview had dealt with his controversial experiments in genetic engineering and, although Charity felt sympathetic to him as a person, she had believed it right from a moral point of view to focus on the dangers of artificially altering life patterns.

The Press had seized upon the story, pseudo-scientific journalists portraying a whole range of grim possibilities that could result from Dr Mitchell's work, from mutant bacteria which could trigger off new diseases to genetically-engineered supermen which totalitarian regimes could produce in line with the old Nazi experiments in breeding a master race.

As a result of the furore a Government commission was set up to inquire into the question and, following its findings, a moratorium was imposed upon Mitchell's work. Now, in this bitter letter, Paul Mitchell had blamed her for drawing public attention to the negative side of his experiments. Sitting in the quiet old church Charity did not need to reread the scrawled handwriting to be disturbed by his words.

'Part of my programme was devoted to engineering a new strain of rice – perhaps you will remember the part you played in having it curtailed when you read of the next famine in Bangladesh,' he had written. 'Not that I am the first scientist to be hampered by prejudice. Pasteur had similar criticism when he tried to introduce inoculation. What disappoints me is that I had believed you possessed a more positive mind.'

It was that last sentence which hurt Charity most. From her brief acquaintance with Paul Mitchell she had found him very attractive and she was depressed that what might have been a warm friendship had foundered like this. Now she wondered if there was anything that she could do to redress the situation . . .

Suddenly there was a crash as the massive church door was flung open. Startled out of her reverie, Charity saw a wild-looking youth in motorcycle leathers stagger up the aisle towards the altar. His crash-helmet with a darkened visor added a bizarre touch.

'Take it back,' he shouted in a strong Derbyshire accent. 'I knew I done wrong to take it . . . I don't want no part of it no more.'

He reached into a zippered pocket, then flung a small

object on to the altar. For a fraction of a second it sparkled as it passed through a ray of wintry sunlight. He turned and, with the sound of sobs coming from behind the tinted visor, reeled between the rows of pews.

Charity half rose to help him, then sank back against the stonework as the church door burst open for the second time and four men appeared, two motorcycle policemen and two ambulance men.

'Come quietly, Hudson,' one of the policemen said. 'You know we'll be able to help you . . . '

'I've given it back. Honest. I didn't take anything else.'

Unregarded in her corner, Charity watched as the ambulance men advanced on the youth. He swung his head from side to side like a trapped animal, then in desperation he plunged past them towards the door. One of the policemen put out his foot and sent him sprawling. In the following struggle he slipped out of his leather jacket and for a moment was free, then a gloved hand seized him by the shirt.

It tore down the middle and for a second Charity glimpsed his white, hairless torso – then he was dragged out. The policemen followed, one with the jacket held at arm's length. The door slammed and Charity was alone again. It had all taken place in a matter of seconds, and might have been a hallucination had it not been for the glint of gold on the altar.

'Flowerland Services,' answered a cool feminine voice.

Desmond Krogh smiled into the telephone mouthpiece and said with elaborate enunciation, 'Good evening, madam. I am one of your VIP clients. Put me through to your exotic blooms department.'

'Exotic is engaged. Please give me your number and you will be called back.'

Thirty seconds later the gold-tinted telephone chirruped and the same feminine voice said,

'Exotic Blooms – your account number, please.'

'Seven-eight-six. I require a special delivery this evening.'

'Certainly, sir. Have you anything specific in mind? To-night we can supply an African Violet, a French Marigold or – if you prefer something less *outré* – we have a fine specimen of English Rose . . . '

'She would be just right.'

'Certainly. And will there be any extra requirements? There can be such floral additions as Venus' Fly Trap, Jack-in-the-Pulpit, Cockspur . . . or perhaps your taste runs to Lady's-Slipper, Golden Rod or even Love-Lies-Bleeding?'

'I don't need extras,' chuckled Desmond Krogh, 'provided the specimen does not wilt. When can I expect delivery?'

'Where to, sir?'

'Concorde Hotel, Alcock Suite.'

'In two hours, sir. Will it be Access or American Express?'

Desmond Krogh rubbed his plump hands together and did a brief soft-shoe shuffle in the centre of the luxurious carpet. Through his floor-to-ceiling window he saw the lights of an aircraft hauling itself into the mauve sky above Heathrow Airport, and his spirits soared with it. Whenever he pulled off a deal he rewarded himself with a treat such as this. The cheque in his wallet generated a glow of confidence and he felt deliciously powerful as he turned to a bottle with a Napoleonic motif on its label.

Punctually at nine o'clock a minicab driver halted his Nippon-Leyland at the Concorde Hotel's canopied entrance.

'Thanks, Three-six-zero,' said Audrey, giving him a handful of one-pound coins while he held the door open for her. As she swept through the lobby, male eyes swivelled to her figure outlined by an expensively plain cocktail dress beneath a silver shoulder cape. Women also stared, envious of the natural fair hair whose soft curls framed a perfect complexion and gave her an expression of haunting innocence. Now that the 'English Look' was in vogue they decided that she could only be a model.

A minute later the door of the Alcock Suite opened to her discreet knock and she commanded her face to smile when she saw the bulky figure of Krogh and caught a gust of his Stud aftershave.

Why me? she fumed inwardly. Why do I always land these pot-gutted macho-merchants?

Aloud she said demurely, 'Good evening, sir. I'm Miss Rose.'

'Come in. You see, I have something waiting for you.' He twirled a bottle of Moet in an ice bucket while his eyes assessed her possibilities. Her 'upper class' clothes, her air of breeding combined with a hint of submissiveness before his masculinity, satisfied him. He granted her his special smile.

'You look as though you have something to celebrate,' she said as she sank on to a large yielding sofa, giving him a look that was bright, eager and wholly professional.

'Oh yes, indeed, Rose.' His voice slurred slightly and she was not surprised to see a half-empty brandy bottle. 'Today I have pulled off a million-pound deal.'

She raised her champagne glass to the third million-pound deal she had been subjected to that month.

'What do you think I am, Rose?' he demanded, drink spilling on to his Cardin tie.

A creep of the first water, screamed a rebellious voice within her head, but audibly she said, 'Without doubt you must be in business . . . oh, do excuse me,' she added as she stifled a sneeze. 'It must be the air-conditioning.'

'But cannot you guess what business?'

Audrey regarded him reflectively, her moist lips parted and her eyes grave as though enumerating his finer points. She had worked for Flowerland long enough to know that with such clients it was not so much a question of hiring out her body as providing the background for an ego-trip.

'Well, you seem to be a man who knows exactly what he wants and makes sure he gets it. So I think you are in something very competitive . . .'

'How right you are!' cried Desmond Krogh, charmed. 'You've got it in one. I'm a film producer.'

'That's just what I was going to say. Oh, lucky me! Tell me the name of one of your films.'

'There have been so many but you might not know them – uh – they have different titles in different countries . . .'

Audrey knew better than to pursue the point. In fact, the

man smirking with self-satisfaction opposite her had never actually produced a film – his talent lay in persuading the screen-struck to finance films which, with the passage of time, dissolved like mirages on the desert air. He had just obtained a new partner in the projected blockbuster *Nympho Planet*, a retired property developer who, having made his financial commitment, was now anxious to contribute his expertise in the casting sessions.

For the next half hour Desmond Krogh tried to press champagne on the girl while regaling her with what he considered were fascinating accounts of his cleverness in manipulating the film world. Film stars and famous directors were referred to by nickname, often with a knowing wink, and there were hints that an actress whose name was at that moment spelled out in lights in Leicester Square had succumbed to his charms . . . and she was evidently not the first lady of the screen to lead him to her bed!

Suddenly he paused, having just offered her a part in his next picture.

'You do not seem keen,' he accused her.

'I'm sorry,' said Audrey, whose reactions had slowed under the egocentric onslaught. 'It's just that to a girl like me, someone like you is a little overpowering.'

'Ah, that's good – you will soon find out if I am overpowered,' he said as he sank beside her on the sofa. 'You will see what sort of a man I am.'

'I'm sure . . . ' began Audrey in her professional voice, but she stopped as she felt his hand, its stubby fingers hooked like claws, slide up the inside of her thigh, brutally probing, while with his other he tugged at the neckline of her dress. She had no time to force herself to respond and he demanded, 'Is that the best you can do? You are not excited . . . you toffee-nosed bitches are all the same!'

'I was so interested in what you were saying,' she said. 'Look, it'll be much more fun if we get undressed properly . . . '

She wriggled free from his grasp, stood up and passed him a drink. Then she turned down the lighting and stood with her back to the window, a slender silhouette against the glow of the airport. His head swayed as he watched her gracefully slip out of her clothes.

'Cold, dry whore,' he muttered as he fumbled with his own clothing. 'You just put on an act for the money. Well, Dezzie Krogh always gets his money's worth, an' tonight I shall even if I have to . . . '

'Of course you will, Mr Krogh,' she said soothingly, her eyes drawn to what he was doing with his hands. 'But – do you suffer from a problem?'

'Problem? Me? You crazy? Ask any of those bitches who've starred in my films!'

'It'll be better if we go into the bedroom,' she said wearily. 'I'm sure you'll manage there – in a nice big bed.'

Staring at her body in the diffused orange light, he struggled to his feet, his expensive trousers slipping to an untidy heap about his ankles. After his boasting the spectacle was too much for her and she could not control a snort of laughter as she walked naked into the next room.

It was the sound of this laughter which penetrated Krogh's befuddled thoughts – the girl was not showing him respect. She was mocking a VIP client . . . for a moment his hand reached towards the telephone. He'd ring Flowerland and that would be the end of her on the game. Another thought struck him. There was a better way.

He stumbled into the bedroom where she lay spread-eagled provocatively on the bed. He threw himself forward, covering her with his heavy body, gripping her arms and gazing into that innocent face which was almost ghostly in the dim light.

'I'll teach you,' he mouthed. 'And it'll be no good yelling rape.'

'Rape does not come into it, Mr Krogh,' said Audrey. 'You are paying for your fun.'

Beside her ear his mouth formed obscenities learned a lifetime ago in school playgrounds, but after some minutes the note of desperation in his voice rose. When he pushed himself up on his arms she felt tears splash on her breast.

'What's wrong, Mr Krogh?' She did not attempt to conceal the contempt which crept into her voice. 'Forgotten to take your ginseng?'

'Bitch, it's the effect you have on me – you do not appreciate me.'

His arm swung and his hand caught her on the side of the head.

'Sadism is extra, Mr Krogh,' she said with ice in her voice.

He collapsed beside her on the bed, his ego momentarily deflated. The rise and fall of her chest became regular, and the thought that she was going to sleep filled him with frustrated panic.

'Please, please, let me try again,' he muttered miserably, reaching out to her. She ignored him as she drew an involuntary breath followed by a sneeze.

'*Gesundheit*,' he responded automatically.

2

Radio City news, folks, and speculation is mounting that the Volkstadt germ warfare panic could spell a serious set-back for the Cabinet. With Britain likely to pull out of the Common Market after the New Year referendum, the new Government has been seeking closer trade links with Eastern Europe, especially East Germany. Any truth in rumours of a bacteriological disaster there will embarrass the Foreign Secretary who has been the architect of the Anglo-East German Friendship Treaty because East Germany is a signatory to the 1983 international agreement banning the production of micro-organisms harmful to human life.

F A Cupholders Tottenham Hotspur will be hard put to field a team at White Hart Lane this weekend as player after player has gone down with flu . . .

Desmond Krogh trembled with inexplicable excitement as he approached the cream and gold doors at the end of the softly-carpeted hotel corridor. Unseen hands drew them back so that an ever-widening band of pink light illuminated his Czarist uniform. He stepped into a magnificent room and saw that the roseate glow came from candelabra whose silverwork flowed into erotic motifs. Pastel silks fell in graceful loops from the centre of the ceiling to damasked walls, giving the effect of a pavilion worthy of Scheherazade. But what captured his attention was the circular bed covered with white nylon fur – similar to one he had seen in pride of place at the Slumberease Supermarket – which stood on a dais under a canopy of mink.

Reclining against its cushions, like the favoured concubine of an oriental despot, was a lovely young woman whose glamorous gown (direct from the Norti-Nites discount warehouse) revealed enough to set his pulse racing.

'Rose of Flowerland, let me try again,' he cried.

'Of course,' she answered, spreading her arms in a languorous gesture and moving her knee so that his throat parched at the thought of what he could almost see. His fingers fumbled with his gilt buttons and his decorations clinked.

'Do you remember Davidson?' she asked softly, as she allowed her gown to slip from her breasts.

Why the hell does she have to mention him? he fumed inwardly as he struggled to kick off his gleaming riding boots.

'He was a partner of mine,' he replied, unbuckling his sword belt. 'He . . . he cheated me . . . he planned it so that I was left without money when our company had to go bankrupt. He just vanished, probably to Australia.'

In reality Henry Davidson vanished after Krogh informed him that as the company would be going bankrupt there would be no way of repaying his investment, or of saving his family home from the official receiver. Tough luck, but that's show business!

The girl on the bed now knelt forward and slowly, ever so slowly, drew her see-through gown above her head and let it whisper down on to the nylon fur.

'Come, Mr Krogh, I'm sure you'll manage this time. Did

you ever find out what happened to Davidson?'

'Naw, forget him.'

He mounted the dais and reached towards the tantalising body, his gaze travelling greedily from her thighs, up the flat, youthful belly, over her breasts to her face . . .

Her face!

She no longer had one. It was as though a wax head had been held in front of a fire, its features melting and seething and then setting in a new mould, a carnival-monster mask the colour of a dead fish. The fair curls had become lank strands of black hair. The ears had just gone apart from a few strips of bleached tissue. Instead of a left eye there was an empty socket, a black tunnel into a decomposing brain. The mouth was lipless, exposing unnaturally long teeth from which trailed a length of dark green waterweed.

'Now you know,' said Davidson, and the form on the bed, which was still the body of Miss Rose of Flowerland though glistening with water, arched to embrace Desmond Krogh . . .

He awoke with his own screaming echoing in his ears. For a moment he believed he was still in the wet clasp of that thing from his delirious dream, then he realized that the bed clothes were soaking with his own sweat. The opening of his eyes was difficult – they must be inflamed, his head ached as though a wedge had been driven into its centre, while his back pained him in sympathy. He remembered that the night before he'd felt feverish and, afraid he'd got a touch of flu, fortified himself with a tumbler of Remy Martin. Now there was no doubt that he was seriously ill. He must get help! With his wife recovering from her latest breakdown in a Surrey nursing home he was alone in the house. He turned to the bedside telephone and tried to focus on the panel of numbered buttons, but instead he saw the drowned face which had turned an excitingly erotic dream into a hellish nightmare.

A spasm in his abdomen halted his efforts and he knew he had to get to the lavatory fast. He rolled out of bed and swayed towards the bathroom, but he was only halfway there when he felt hot liquid gush down his legs.

Sobbing with humiliation he collapsed on all fours and crawled the rest of the distance, leaving a dark trail across the white carpet. As he moved a jolt of agony caught him in the groin and it took all his determination to reach for the bottle from which he had taken his nightcap and swallow several mouthfuls of brandy. The spirit gave him strength and he hauled himself to his feet by means of a heated towel rail.

He unfastened his fetid pyjama pants and stepped out of them. The next moment he stared in terror as he caught sight of himself in a tinted wall mirror. Across his sagging stomach was a rash of haemorrhage spots and lower down a purple swelling the size of an orange protruded from his hairy groin.

'I'm poxed, the bitch has poxed me,' he howled, hammering at the mirror until his knuckles left bloody smears on the glass. Then, as his mind clouded, a manic surge of energy galvanised his body and he hurled himself out of the house and into the quiet Pinner street.

'There he goes,' yelled PC Scott as the Panda car swung round a corner into a residential avenue. The policewoman at the wheel laughed as she put her foot down.

'He looks sweet,' she said as the car accelerated past leafless cherry trees. 'Just like the old girl's description – starkers apart from his pyjama jacket.'

'I'll jump him when we get alongside. Be ready with the blanket.'

A moment later PC Scott brought Desmond Krogh down to the pavement with a rugby tackle.

'What is he – a drunk or a pervert?' called the policewoman taking a folded blanket from the boot.

'I think he must be sick,' said the constable, sinking on one knee and reaching for Desmond Krogh's pulse.

Suddenly the prone man gave a shriek that brought householders to their gates. The policeman's face became bloodless and sweat sheened his forehead as he saw that where the purple swelling had split evil coloured pus was spurting.

'Call an ambulance quick,' he shouted.

'What's wrong with him?' the WPC asked as she reached through the car window for the radio microphone.

PC Scott threw the blanket over the victim and backed away.

'Bloody Germans,' he muttered.

The sad-faced messenger opened the leather-lined door, ushered through the tall old man in the disgraceful tweeds and closed it reverently before heading for the staff washroom for a surreptitious smoke. Inside the spacious oak-panelled office Peter Barnet, the suave Chief Medical Officer for the Greater London Council, took charge of the introductions with professional aplomb.

'Minister, allow me to present Sir Robert McAusland, our leading epidemiologist. Indeed, it would be no exaggeration to say the world's leading . . . '

'Morning, Minister,' said Sir Robert in his soft voice which retained a Scottish burr. 'Morning, John,' he added to the Permanent Under-Secretary for Health.

From behind his vast desk, the Health Minister David Crisp extended a plump hand and then waved to a club armchair. His jowls had become prominent too early, his hair had thinned before its time but his eyes retained a look of youthful determination, and when he sucked in his lips – which he tended to do when confronted by photographers – he achieved an expression of reassuring stubbornness. After the recent election he had hoped for Defence in order to preside over Britain's nuclear disarmament, but the Prime Minister had pleaded with him to accept the challenge of sorting out the chaos of an underfinanced National Health Service.

'Thanks for coming at such short notice,' he said as Sir Robert sank back against soft bottle-green leather.

'It isn't the first time I've been here,' replied the old man. 'I've sat in this chair and done my best to explain Lassa Fever and Legionnaires' Disease . . . ' He glanced at the book-lined walls, the watercolour seascapes and the pile of red dispatch boxes on a Chippendale table. 'Governments come and go, but the sanctums of power don't alter,' he mused.

'This government is going to be here for a while,' said the Minister briskly. 'Please,' he added as Sir Robert produced a silver tobacco box with an enquiring look. He watched with silent fascination as the slender fingers of the old doctor rolled a cigarette and inserted it in the corner of his mouth, explaining the yellow stain on his otherwise snowy beard.

'You know what we want from you, Sir Robert?'

'Ay, a run down on bubonic plague, no doubt in regard to that Volkstadt business.'

'The Minister needs to have a clear, non-technical picture,' said the Under-Secretary.

'In a couple of hours my Cabinet colleagues will be grilling me,' said the Minister with his frank laugh.

Sir Robert lounged back and drew on his misshapen cigarette reflectively.

'It's a curious aspect of human nature that men are so preoccupied with political intrigue and war that they ignore the natural forces which really shape their destinies,' he said. 'The First World War claimed about eight and a half million lives, yet in 1918 influenza was responsible for twenty million deaths. That world epidemic is hardly mentioned in history books, and as yet no cure has been found for influenza . . . '

'Nor has one been found for war,' interrupted the Minister drily. 'But do go on, Sir Robert, as briefly as possible, please. Before long there may be a division on the Universal Fingerprinting Bill.'

'Then I'll cut out the philosophy and keep to the facts,' said Sir Robert. 'Historical background first. One of the earliest references to what we think of as plague is mentioned in the first chapter of the Book of Samuel as afflicting the Philistines. It's interesting because the mortality of mice – which in all probability were rats – was mentioned in conjunction with the pestilence which must have occurred around 350 BC.

'Europe was first stricken by bubonic plague in the sixth century AD when the whole of the Roman world was affected, including the north coast of Africa.

'In England St Bede described several outbreaks of

disease between 664 and 683 which are likely to have been bubonic plague, though we can't be certain. Retrospective diagnosis depends on whether any description of buboes was included in contemporary accounts.

'Our first real knowledge of the devastation caused by plague came in the fourteenth century with the Black Death, so called because of its necrotic symptoms.'

'Necrotic?' asked the Minister, looking up from the green scribbling pad on which he had sketched an ivy-covered tombstone.

'The skin turns black,' Sir Robert explained. 'The Black Death was the most powerful epidemic ever recorded and it affected Western history more than any other factor before or since. Social structures changed overnight. In England the shortage of labour awakened the working man to his value in the community for the first time so it was the death knell for feudalism as well as a third of the population. In London alone 100,000 died, half of them being buried in Smithfield.'

'Was it one great outbreak?'

'No, there were a series of outbreaks in quick succession.' Sir Robert produced some neatly folded notes. 'It first came in 1348, then again in 1361 and 1369. It originated in Central Asia and spread to China where it was estimated thirteen million people died. In the whole of the East the death toll reached thirty-seven million, while Hecker has calculated that in Europe twenty-five million perished of bubonic and pneumonic plague – I'll explain the differences later.

'Although outbreaks of plague recurred on the Continent during the fifteenth, sixteenth and seventeenth centuries, England remained free until 1664 when the Great Plague of London began.'

'The Great Fire cleansed the Plague from London, didn't it?' asked the Minister, continuing to doodle.

'That's a popular belief. In fact the plague was really over before the fire, just as it had subsided spontaneously in other cities. That's one of the mysteries of plague – for no apparent reason it will vanish. By the end of the seventeenth century plague had virtually disappeared from

Europe. An exception to this was in Marseilles in 1720 when there was an outbreak following the arrival of a ship from the Levant on which several people had died of plague during the voyage. Bales of cloth from its cargo were smuggled out of quarantine and as a result forty thousand people died from the infection.'

Afraid that the old man would ramble on about the historical aspects, the Minister interjected, 'What about the present day situation, Sir Robert? Any recent outbreaks?'

'In Europe, just after the Second World War, there were outbreaks in Taranto in Italy and Ajaccio in Corsica, but with a relatively high standard of hygiene in Europe, quarantine regulations and the control of rats – remember those metal disks they used to put on ships' mooring lines to prevent the vermin coming ashore? – we seem to have eliminated the threat.'

'You say – *seem* to have eliminated the threat,' said Peter Barnet. 'Surely there is no chance that there could be an epidemic of plague in Britain?'

Sir Robert shrugged.

'If you believed that I wouldn't be sitting here. In 1878 there was an outbreak in Russia, near Vetlianka, which put the European governments into a panic. They sent commissions to study and help control the pestilence, and it was found that this area around the Volga was an old breeding ground of the disease. Today the Soviet authorities withhold information as to whether or not these conditions remain. In the past, lands that are now part of the USSR were responsible for the pestilence spreading east and west.'

David Crisp began another tombstone on his scribbling block and Sir Robert paused to roll himself another cigarette.

'What we think of as plague takes three clinical forms – pneumonic, septicemic and bubonic, the latter condition taking its name from the word buboe which means an inflammatory swelling of lymph nodes. This became famous during the Great Plague of London as the plague mark.'

The Minister began jotting down notes.

'In the old days any virulent disease which caused widespread death was regarded as plague, but what we are talking about is an infectious fever caused by *Pasteurella pestis* or *Yersinia pestis* which is basically a disease of rodents, but which causes epidemics in humans when passed on to them by the rodents' fleas.

'When man is infected by *Pasteurella pestis* it takes the three clinical forms I have mentioned.

'In past epidemics it is the bubonic form which has made up about three quarters of the total cases, and laymen often refer to *Pasteurella pestis* as bubonic plague without realising that it is merely one form of it. From the moment of infection the incubation period can be as short as thirty-six hours. Speech then slurs, there are muscular tremors, the tongue swells, subcutaneous haemorrhages cause skin discoloration and the patient may hallucinate. The temperature tends to fall on the second or third day, and when the usual constipation is followed by diarrhoea it is a very bad sign.

'To begin with, plague is hard to diagnose as the only visible symptom to go on is the appearance of buboes, usually in the region of the groin or armpit, but also in the cervical, submaxillary or femoral glands. Usually they suppurate, discharging pus after bursting under pressure, sometimes with severe loss of blood. Death usually comes on the fifth day.

'Often the effect on the patient is to make him appear as though he is in an extreme fit of delirium tremens.

'Septicemic plague occurs when the bacillus is injected by a flea directly into the bloodstream, causing the patient to die within twenty-four hours.

'Finally we have pneumonic plague which we read about in accounts of the old epidemics. As the name suggests, it is the lungs which are affected. Its onset is fast, the face blackens and breathing may go up to sixty respirations per minute. As the illness progresses, large amounts of bloody sputum are coughed up seething with plague bacilli.'

'So the spread of plague depends on fleas leaving infected rats and infecting humans,' said the Minister.

Sir Robert shook his head.

'Sorry, no. Remember the outbreak in Marseilles I mentioned – there the germs were carried in cloth. Pneumonic plague is passed from man to man through the breath.'

He looked at his notes.

'According to Price, the ideal conditions for the spread of pneumonic plague are "Cold or freezing conditions with relative high humidity (such as occur when people crowd together in a hard winter)." Rather like the weather conditions we are having now,' he added with a smile at the Minister.

'The point about plague is its amazing virulence. In laboratory tests mice have been fatally infected by as few as three bacilli. These bacilli are remarkably resilient, they remain alive in dried sputum for at least three months and in infected organs held in laboratory conditions have retained their potency for ten years.

'Because plague is so highly infectious and brings death so swiftly, it has been a favourite of the bacteriological warfare boffins along with anthrax. If there is any truth in the rumours about Volkstadt it is most likely to be a newly developed strain of *Pasteurella pestis*. By "newly developed" I mean a mutant strain, perhaps achieved by genetic engineering, which would be resistant to our conventional serums.'

Sir Robert let a silence follow his words in a way that always proved so effective in his lectures.

'What is the answer to conventional plague?' asked the Under-Secretary.

'Well, John, people can be vaccinated against plague with antigens made from killed virulent plague bacilli, but this does not guarantee freedom from infection. Once a patient is known to have plague antibiotic treatment can be effective – streptomycin, terramycin and aureomycin – but it must be administered early. And here is the problem. In isolated cases plague is difficult to diagnose in the early stages. It can be confused with influenza and there may be no clinical signs from which diagnosis can be made. Therefore bacteriological examinations are essential and this means microscopic examination of pus or sputum and serum hemagglutination, agglutination and complement fixation tests . . . '

The Minister laid down his ballpoint. The technicalities meant nothing to him but the expression on his face showed he appreciated Sir Robert's gloomy message.

'Such tests take time, and those handling the patients, especially those with pneumonic plague, are in extreme danger of being infected. Text books lay down that doctors and nurses in contact with pneumonic plague suspects must be protected by complete overalls, gloves, face masks of eight layers of gauze covered by a deflection mask, and *hoods equipped with goggles*. Those who have had contact with the suspect must be quarantined for seven days and chemoprophylaxis with sulfadiazine should be instituted.'

He removed the soggy butt of his cigarette and beamed about him.

'I hope that tells you what you want to know, gentlemen. Thankfully the west has escaped the attentions of the plague for the last three hundred years, otherwise Europe would be the Third World today. Plague is ninety per cent fatal and a return of the Black Death could have meant that man might not have reached the moon or even developed things we take for granted such as electricity.'

Peter Barnet regarded the old man quizzically, but he wagged his nicotine-stained finger at him. 'Think about it. Supposing three-quarters of the population of Britain and Europe had been swept away towards the end of the last century when there was no effective answer to pandemics – what sort of world do you think we would be living in now?'

He smiled brightly having made this point and then thought of another.

'It is an interesting speculation,' he said. 'If plague were to appear in London on the same scale as it did in 1665, on the basis of London's present population, over a million and a half people would die, and that would mean disposing of well over seven thousand tons of infected flesh.'

3

. . . and that was The Strippers' chart-topping videodisc single 'Lady Santa,' and this is Phil Jason bringing you the best of listening from Radio City. Before our next spin, here is Newsflash. *At the United Nations East Germany is expected to make a full statement about the reported leak of harmful germs from a laboratory at Volkstadt which is said to be involved in lethal bacteriological experiments. In Westminster the Opposition will take the opportunity to pressure the Government over Britain's friendship treaty with East Germany in view of germ warfare allegations.*

Anyone watching Charity Brown slide from behind the wheel of her white Mercedes convertible and enter the Park Lane Hilton would have been astonished to learn that beneath her voluminous mink she felt her stomach was swarming with butterflies. She was about to have lunch with The Digger – and five years of hard work and hard scheming would reach its climax.

With a bland smile the Chinese receptionist welcomed her to Trader Vic's and reverently passed her coat to a Filipino waiter to be checked.

'I have a luncheon appointment with Mr Victor Kelly,' said Charity.

'Ah yes, Mr Victor Kelly,' said the receptionist in the cheong-sam, doing what Charity mentally regarded as her 'ethnic bit'. 'Please to come this way.'

In the gloaming of the exotic restaurant Charity saw Vic Kelly, a tall glass in his hand, lounging back against palm-frond matting while above his blond head a large tiki carving gazed down with paua-shell eyes. He was a tall bulky man who had an everlasting rumpled look despite the

Savile Row suits which he felt befitted the managing-director of Radio City.

On glimpsing Charity his broad pink face was split by a friendly grin and, as he hauled himself to his feet, he said in his unmistakable accent, 'Great to see yer, girl.' His pale eyes approved her oyster-coloured silk dress and matching hat whose broad brim threw a mysterious shadow over the upper half of her face. He knew that her female colleagues at the station privately mocked her untrendy elegance – referring to her as The Princess – but he also knew that this elegance was remembered when their jeans and sweat shirts had ceased to suggest anything except dull conformity.

'Thirst things first,' he said jovially. 'What'll yer drink? Last time you went for the Maui Fizz . . . '

Charity glanced down the list of drinks with evocative Polynesian and Caribbean names.

'A Zombie,' she said. 'After my trip to darkest Derbyshire I feel like one.'

The Chinese girl nodded and departed with a flash of ivory thigh.

'Well, Princess . . . ' Vic leaned his arms on the bamboo table between them and treated her to his candid look – a look which his many enemies compared unfavourably to that directed by a rattlesnake at a hypnotised rabbit.

'Well, Digger?' responded Charity, determined not to yield her boss the slightest advantage. 'What's that concoction you're drinking?'

'A Suffering Bastard.'

'Yes, you look as though a pick-me-up would help.'

'Yeah, I'm a bit captain in my comic. Guess I've got a flu bug. Half the station is down with it.'

'I do love your Australianisms – what's that one supposed to mean?'

'That's simple. Captain – Captain Cook – crook. Comic – Comic Cuts – guts. I'm crook in my guts.'

'Does your responsibility for the King's English ever worry you?'

'I leave that to the likes of you,' he said with his deceptively boyish laugh. Before leaving Australia Vic Kelly had clawed himself a name in commercial radio, and after arriving in London he had done the same, his ruthlessness camouflaged by a Sydney accent and a certain rough charm.

'Now Charity, one of my little birds tells me . . .'

'Shall we discuss your little bird after we've ordered?' said Charity, taking a menu from a suitably inscrutable waiter. 'Spare ribs to start with, and then the butterfly steak.'

'They must have bloody big butterflies . . . Charlie Chan, I'll have the ribs and then an Outrigger salad.'

While they waited for their meal Vic started on another Suffering Bastard and gossiped about the station.

'Had a D-Notice in this morning,' he said. 'Haven't had any for a while. Fair took me back to the old Wilson days – then they used to whistle down Fleet Street like they were being fired from a belt-fed mortar. Remember the ruckus about them?'

'Hardly – my only interests were netball and elocution lessons in those days. What did this one prohibit?'

Her question was interrupted by the arrival of the first course. Later, while they were dabbling their fingers in the lemon-scented finger bowls, Charity said, 'Whatever your little bird told you is probably right, Vic. I've been offered an interviewing job on TV. It could lead to my own show.'

'But you have your own show with us.'

'But why should I hide my looks from my audience? This may come as a surprise to a radio buff like you, but the thing about TV is that people can actually see you – in colour, and soon in hologram.'

'The word "colour" suggests something. Is this a blow for the minorities? Do you want to give a fillip to your soul brothers and sisters? See folks, black is beautiful – and articulate.'

Charity shook her head emphatically.

'You know it's not that. I have no hang-ups about being black. I don't need to play the West Indian like someone not a million miles from here likes to play the dinkum Aussie . . . '

'Touché.'

'The Race Game means nothing to me. I am *me* period and *me* is going to the top. And it seems I've gone as far as I can go with Radio City – it's been a good ride and I'm grateful.'

'You're taking a risk, girl. They may only want you as a token to impress the IBA, and after a few shows the novelty could wear off . . . '

'No way. You should see the contract I've been offered. And you know I could do it well enough.'

'Oh sure. Providing you don't let your erratic love life snarl you up, you'll be fine. You can hide things in front of a mike that you can't in front of a camera.'

'Well, there's no erratic love life at the moment so that isn't an immediate problem.'

'Guess folk are going to miss you. A lot of our listeners are black and you mean a great deal to them – much more than reggae music sessions. You showed them that it could be done.'

'Well, I'll be showing them even more on TV, won't I? Now, I understand my contract with City expires at the end of the month . . . '

'Jeez, behind those doe-like eyes there's a mind that would make a computer look sentimental. But I get your drift – how much do you want to stay?'

'What I want is not a salary increase . . .'

'Well, that's original. What is it?'

'A seat on the board.'

'Stone the crows!' Vic exploded, reaching for his glass. 'You want what? How about my job while you're at it?'

'That'll come later.'

He regarded her solemnly.

'You are one helluva Sheila! OK, I'll try and talk the chairman and the board into it. I can't promise . . . '

Charity fought not to let him see her triumph.

'You know you can bully them into anything,' she said. 'Tell them it'll look good to have a black lady on the board.'

'Hey, I thought you said . . . ' He suddenly began to laugh and signalling a waiter he ordered a bottle of champagne.

'We ought to celebrate – one of us has done something

clever, and maybe we both have.'

When it arrived Vic asked, 'How's the latest programme working out?'

'I want to talk to you about that because something very odd happened when I was at Eyam yesterday.' And she began to describe the events which had taken place in the church.

'What was it he threw on the altar?' asked Vic.

Charity opened her handbag and drew out a gold chain from which hung a golden cross decorated with moonstones. He took it from her and peered closely at the symbol engraved on its centre:

'You're taking a chance hanging on to this, aren't you?' he said.

'Call it evidence – it's a seventeenth-century anti-plague amulet,' said Charity. 'When the men dragged him out his shirt tore and I think I saw something which I can't quite believe . . . he had a purple blotch beneath his armpit.'

'So he had a birthmark?'

'Or what used to be termed a bubo . . . '

'Stone the crows, girl. That D-Notice . . . it was an indefinite embargo on any stories about an infectious disease called . . . hang on . . .' He fumbled through his pockets and finally produced a piece of paper. '. . . a disease called *Pasteurella pestis*. I thought it referred to the germ warfare scare, but I've just realised what it really is.'

Charity looked at him with widening eyes.

'The Black Death, sweetheart, the Black bloody Death!'

It seemed as though time had stood still in the Health Minister's office. Twenty-four hours had passed since Sir Robert had scattered his cigarette ash on the Wilton carpet, but the three men were in their exact positions of the previous day. The gloomy silence was broken only when a white telephone on a side table gave a deferential bleep. The Under-Secretary picked up the handset, listened a moment and passed it over to the Chief Medical Officer.

'For you, Peter,' he said in the tone of one expecting the worst.

Peter Barnet grunted into the mouthpiece several times, then said, 'Repeat that slowly, I can't believe what you're telling me.'

The others gazed at him as though trying to decipher the worry lines etched across his forehead. After a minute he said, 'I'll get back to you shortly, but meanwhile not a hint – not a single bloody hint – of this must get out. Influenza, man, blame Super flu! Yes, a new and highly virulent strain!'

With a bemused look he put down the telephone, uttered two words of ultimate blasphemy and shook his head as though trying to clear his mind.

'Sorry, Minister,' he said. 'That was confirmation that the suspect cases are positive. There is plague in London.'

'From Volkstadt?' the Under-Secretary demanded.

'Damn it, we won't be able to carry the country into the alliance if this gets out,' David Crisp muttered. His hand scuttled towards the red telephone on his desk. 'I must warn the PM immediately.'

'Your treaty is not in danger,' the health chief said wearily. 'But the real explanation is so fantastic the public may not buy it.'

'Tell us, man,' said the Minister, his hand moving from the telephone.

'The pathologist at Coppett's Wood Hospital confirms what we feared. Four cases with fever symptoms which were taken there had plague. A couple were dead on arrival, a patient from Pinner is in a coma but the fourth, who had been taken ill in Streatham, was able to tell us something. He had been working on a City building site with the two men who died. The stupid bastards plundered a plague pit.'

'Do you seriously expect me to tell the Cabinet that we're faced with an outbreak of plague because some three-hundred-year-old crypt has been opened?' exploded the Minister. 'If I were you I'd be very concerned about the integrity of my advisers. If we were to mention plague pits in the House, the Opposition would scream "Whitewash!" And I wouldn't blame them.'

He sucked in his lips.

'The way I see it is – if bubonic plague has been diagnosed in London it can only have come in from abroad. I'm sure that when your department has checked *thoroughly* it'll be found that the virus was brought in by a human carrier from some Third World country where outbreaks still occur – ah – let's say India or Uganda.'

'The Racial Harmony people wouldn't like that one,' the Under-Secretary pointed out drily.

'Perhaps not. When did Argentina have its last outbreak, I wonder?'

'1940,' said the Under-Secretary. 'I've done a bit of checking in the eventuality of . . . well, such a situation. However, Minister, I must tell you that the notion of plague spreading from a burial ground is not so extraordinary as you might suppose. I'm sure medical opinion could be found to support the hypothesis.'

'Thank you,' said Peter Barnet, his voice cold with suppressed anger at David Crisp's remarks. 'I'm convinced that my advisers are not mistaken. During the great Plague of London huge communal graves were dug in fields round the city once it was found that conventional burial procedures were not adequate. They were filled with corpses to a level of six feet below the surface, from which comes the present law that a coffin must be buried at that depth.

'Most of those pits have remained undisturbed since the seventeenth century. Some were grassed over and left as open spaces – like Knightsbridge Green in Brompton Road – others were built over and forgotten. The bodies interred in them were full of live plague germs. Yesterday we heard Sir Robert say that in laboratories plague bacilli have remained virulent for up to ten years.'

'But we are talking about a period thirty times as long.'

'Certainly, Minister. But if the bacilli can remain in a state of suspended animation for a decade, why not longer? After all, viral organisms in mummies removed from sealed tombs in Egypt have become re-animated . . . '

'Wasn't something like that supposed to have been responsible for Tutankhamen's Curse?'

'It looks as though London has inherited a far more deadly curse,' said the Under-Secretary. 'Those plague pits could be described as the nuclear waste of the Middle Ages.'

'That's it!' cried the Minister with a smile of relief. 'The PM might go for that. Right in line with his atomic policy. The nuclear waste of the Middle Ages. Great!'

'I think you'll find that the Middle Ages ended quite a while before the Great Plague of London,' said Peter Barnet.

'This is no time to be pedantic,' the Minister interjected. 'Remember that Sir Robert said that in the fourteenth century fifty thousand Black Death victims were buried where Smithfield Market now stands . . . '

'Could a suit be filed against the building contractors?' the Under-secretary asked. 'It would add credence to the story.'

'I think so,' Peter Barnet said. 'It's certainly against our by-laws to disturb a graveyard or open a plague crypt or pit without authorisation. In fact, great care has been taken to ensure that they were not disturbed . . . '

'But apparently not enough.'

'Yes, it'll be bloody embarrassing for the GLC to have to admit that a pit was opened,' said the Under-Secretary with an arctic smile. 'A Bacteriological Time-bomb! – I can see the headlines now.'

'Don't let us cry *Plague*! until we have to,' said the

Minister, reaching for the red telephone again. 'Your idea of blaming the flu bug might save the day for us all. I shudder to think of the panic that would follow a rumour of the Black Death returning. With luck the infection may not spread. I take it your people are taking precautions – er – discreetly.'

'Naturally,' retorted Peter Barnet. 'Of the men working on the site only one has vanished, but a search is on and inevitably he'll be found if symptoms break out. The others – including a lad traced to Derbyshire – have been taken into isolation with their families, and I mean *isolation*. Following your advice I have kept the number of my officers aware of the situation to the minimum, and because of the possible germ warfare connection all have signed the Official Secrets Act. I have also contacted the World Health Organisation privately . . . '

'What the hell did you do that for?' cried the Minister. 'We aren't Bangladesh – we don't need foreign aid yet.'

'No, but we may need a hell of a lot of serum and antibiotics. Naturally I see no point in unduly alarming the public, but God help us all if this gets out of control.'

The Under-Secretary smiled cynically.

'Or if the press gets wind of the fact that we are as unprepared for such an eventuality as we are for a nuclear attack.'

'We'll keep the D-Notices in force,' said David Crisp reassuringly. 'Ah, Prime Minister,' he said into the red telephone. 'I have rather good news over the Volkstadt situation. The Health Department has just confirmed several cases of plague, but it comes from a purely local source. Of course, sir, I absolutely agree it would be diplomatically undesirable to admit to the infection while our Eastern friends remain under suspicion. Yes, Prime Minister, a complete clamp-down!'

4

London's Heart and Voice . . .
Bootifool Raa-dee-oh Cit-ee!

Vic Kelly eased his tall frame into Phil Jason's tiny studio as the 'heavenly choir' station identification faded.

'And who thought up that garbage?' the DJ demanded with upturned eyes.

'I did, sport,' hissed The Digger. 'But don't worry, there's plenty more where that came from.'

Turning to see his boss behind him, Jason pushed back his earphones and pointed to the green light indicating they were off-air during a taped appeal for the Iranian Famine Fund.

'Slumming?' he asked.

Vic grinned at him with professional good nature and asked, 'Any new angles on the Volkstadt story?' Jason started one of the twin turntables on his desk, and pointed to a sheet of yellow paper on his news clipboard which Vic read thoughtfully. The stylus came to the end of the record, a red transmission light glowed and the DJ pulled a flexible microphone towards him.

'Wasn't that really something!' he exclaimed with instant enthusiasm. He pressed a button and his klaxon gimmick sounded. 'Well worth a couple of beeps. I really think that . . . ' He frantically scanned a typed list. 'Yes, I really think Aces and Eights are worth an encore. Right? Then keep listening. But first *Newsflash* . . . '

East Germany may invite Western medical observers to Volkstadt to scotch rumours of a germ warfare disaster. The government claims the rumour started when a large number of people were stricken by a new and pernicious form of influenza. The capitalist press is blamed for distorting the story to jeopardise the Anglo-East German friendship treaty.

Here in the capital flu is also the main news. The GLC Health Department has warned Londoners they may be threatened by the same bug which hit Volkstadt.

Peter Barnet, our chief Medical Officer, has issued the following statement: 'If notification of such cases is given quickly to the appropriate health authorities and patients can be isolated there should be no danger of an epidemic. Symptoms to watch for are headaches combined with backaches, feverish trembling, swelling of the tongue and a painless cough bringing up thick sputum tinged with blood . . .'

Ugh!

Should you or one of yours be unfortunate enough to have these symptoms you are asked to phone your local health department immediately – I'll give you the telephone numbers in a moment. Medical Chief Barnet emphasises that this form of flu – nicknamed Super flu – is highly infectious and if you think you have it don't – repeat do not – go to your doctor's waiting room. Ring up and wait in bed for a health visitor or district nurse and you'll be properly taken care of.

So no need to panic, folks. But just in case you get the colliwobbles, it might be an idea to jot down these numbers . . .

Vic closed the sound-proofed studio door behind him and saw the trim outline of Charity Brown in the corridor. A moment later he escorted her into his dove-grey office with its clinical chrome and plastic furniture.

'As promised I had a yarn to the chairman and several Board members about you,' he said as he opened his refrigerated drinks cabinet, pouring an iced sherry for her and opening a can of Foster's beer for himself.

'And have they come to a decision?' asked Charity as she settled decoratively on a white leather couch.

'They want to discuss it among themselves,' he answered. 'I got the weirdo impression they thought I was trying to hustle them. Can't have this colonial fellow telling us what to do, what?'

'I've been asked to do a *Guest Host* show on the telly as a dummy run. You know – the chat show where they have a different compère each week. I'd like to know whether I'll still be with Radio City by then.'

'Good-o, that'll hurry them up. I might add that yours truly is all for you joining the Board, but while this hangs over us the show still has to go on.'

Charity nodded over her sherry.

'Did you get a lead on your bubonic plague story?'

'Just a lot of sincere denials – all a little too sincere.'

'I reckon there's something pretty crook going on. That D-Notice hasn't been rescinded and those so-called Super flu precautions sound like typical pommy bullshit to me.'

'Elegantly phrased, as always, but I do agree with you.'

'Charity, you break the story and I'll get you promoted chairperson of this outfit.'

'Is that a promise? As a matter of fact I am getting on with it. And as I can't get a whisper through my usual sources, I'm going to tackle Dr Paul Mitchell. He just might know something.'

'Isn't he the microbiologist you got labelled Frankenstein? He must hate your guts.'

'I'm sure he does, but he's the only person I can think of. My Voices tell me to try him.'

'You and your Voices,' Vic scoffed.

Back in the corridor Charity saw the over-groomed receptionist waving to her.

'Sounds like one of your soul sisters in trouble,' she said, holding out a telephone receiver.

'Is that Miz Charity Ah'm talking to?' came an agitated voice. 'Ah listen to you a lot, Miz Charity, an' now Ah need your help. Mah man Leroy is dead an' Ah'm goin' crazy . . .'

The proprietor of the Fenny Stratford Boatyard looked up from the incandescent bead at the end of his welding torch as a white Mercedes convertible parked by his workshop.

'Is Dr Mitchell's boat kept here?' called Charity.

'He's the only one who leaves his boat in the water during

the winter,' he replied. He turned off the gas, pushed back his goggles and prepared to have a chat about the eccentricity of a man who enjoyed cruising on the Grand Union Canal in such weather.

'I was told in London he's on his boat,' Charity continued. 'Know where I might find it?'

'I'd say *Blue Flame* is moored about a couple of miles up the Fenny Pound,' said the proprietor, nodding to the narrow sheet of water gleaming dully between desolate fields. 'All you have to do is follow the towpath.' He looked doubtfully at her fashionable white trenchcoat and matching boots. 'Not that you're dressed for it, miss. There's some right muddy patches. He may be back tomorrow.'

'Tomorrow may be too late,' said Charity. 'May I leave my car with you?'

He nodded.

'You wouldn't be the lady with the radio show, would you? I suppose you want to interview the doctor, but don't forget to put in a bit about canal cruising – this business could do with a plug since Luxury Tax came in.'

'Fun afloat and all that,' said Charity with a deceptive smile, but as she squelched along the path beside the leaden water rain washed it away.

In the main cabin of his Freeman cruiser Paul Mitchell looked like a man at peace with his world. On the mahogany table between comfortable locker seats stood an almost empty bottle of Macon beside an open book, and from a pan simmering on the calor stove steamed the aroma of a plain but honest stew. Stereo speakers provided a Sibelius symphony whose soaring portrayal of remote pagan forests fitted in perfectly with his mood.

He had brought the cruiser up the canal to write a paper to be delivered to the Society for the Advancement of Science. Apart from jotting down several alternative titles, he had enjoyed the unique pleasure which comes from rebelling against a work deadline, having temporarily abandoned the project in favour of red wine, music and Simenon detective novel.

The Sibelius came to an end and Paul dozed gently, his long frame sprawled against the dark green upholstery. Fair hair hung over his forehead which, even though his next birthday would be his thirtieth, gave him a boyish look curiously emphasised by the rimless glasses which had slipped down his nose.

It was the bump of someone stepping into the cockpit followed by a rap on the cabin door which made his eyelids flutter open. The Freeman moved slightly as he climbed slowly to his feet and unbolted the door beyond which a tall figure was silhouetted against the louring sky.

'Hello?' he muttered, still only half awake.

'Dr Mitchell, I presume,' said Charity. 'May a poor half-soaked girl come aboard?'

'Oh no, not you!' he cried as he recognised her in the cabin light. 'Will you please do me the biggest favour it is possible for you to do me and just bloody well get lost!'

'Dr Mitchell, I know we have had our differences in the past . . . ' began Charity.

'Dr Frankenstein, if you please,' he said, slumping in his corner seat. 'You know, the guy you stopped from making monsters – incidentally buggering up the most promising genetic engineering programme conceived in this country. Still, it didn't do *your* programme any harm by all accounts!'

'Please listen for a moment,' she pleaded. 'I admit that I emphasised the possible dangers of altering gene structures, but I never expected the story to snowball like it did.'

'Well, snowball it did,' Paul growled. 'How the press loved it! "Bodies without Souls" screamed the *Evening Express*. "Stop this Frankenstein," thundered the *Daily Standard*. Even *The Onlooker* went overboard in an editorial about irresponsible tampering with life and "the possible hazards of genetic engineering techniques in which genes of one organism are inserted into another . . . " And the Sundays – did they have a field day! Articles about benign vegetables being turned into triffids, clone armies of the future. Up it came in Parliament with the do-gooders making pronouncements on the dangers of breeding new viral strains for germ warfare.'

He emptied his glass.

'There was the Rickwood committee of inquiry, and to prove how responsible and humane and right-thinking they are – and to save themselves the research grant – the Government declared a moratorium of genetic engineering until the whole question could be re-examined in the light of fresh data. And how could there be fresh data when our unit had been closed down?'

Charity stood before his wrath, trying to stop her teeth chattering while water dripped from her trenchcoat.

'But you, dear lady, were hailed as a splendid radio journalist and you were given your own show. I understand you got hundreds of letters from people thanking you for saving them from the wicked scientists, and your name was even quoted in *Hansard*. Yet I wonder if you knew what I was engaged on when the moratorium was imposed. I was trying to engineer a long-stemmed form of rice so that when rivers flooded in India the plant would survive by rising with the waters. Hardly the Devil's work, I'd say.'

For the moment he seemed to have talked out his anger. He glared at his empty glass and Charity realised he was slightly drunk.

'I've walked miles along a quagmire of a towpath just to see you,' she said. 'Icy water is trickling inside my coat and I'm freezing to death. I have also brought this peace-offering so I do think you might listen to what I have to say.'

'Tell me one thing,' Paul interrupted. 'If you had the chance to do it over again – would you?'

'It was a good story,' Charity said. 'I'd do it again.'

'Good. That's frank at least,' he said, combing the hair out of his eyes with his fingers. 'And while I don't like *you* any better, I do like your honesty. So as you're aboard you may as well take off your mack and get warm.'

He turned up the stove.

'And what's this about a goodwill gesture?'

'This,' said Charity, and produced a bottle of Old Oak rum from a carrier bag. 'I thought it might be what you canal mariners fought off the cold with.'

'You thought right,' he said. He took out a clean glass for her from a built-in cupboard. 'This'll stop you shivering, and then maybe you'd like to risk some of my hybrid stew . . . '

He poured her a generous tot, and then one equally generous for himself into the empty wine glass.

With the thaw in his mood, coupled with the golden spirit and the cosy interior of the cruiser, Charity felt almost light-hearted. She looked with approval at the ingenious way the builders had included a wardrobe, drawers and a sink beneath a movable worktop in the cabin. At the far end a folding door opened on to a smaller cabin with a bunk on either side. Looking through the rain-speckled window at the darkling world outside, she could understand why Paul Mitchell used it as a retreat from the busy life of an international scientist.

With her glass of Old Oak in her hand, she sat opposite him at the table while he put on a new cassette and soft music filled the cabin.

'So you'd do the story over again,' he mused.

She nodded.

'You might be working for improved crops but that doesn't mean that others could not be producing bacteria resistant to antibiotics more deadly than the neutron bomb . . . '

'In which case it would be best to keep the balance by having our own form of plague . . . '

'It's about plague I want to talk with you.'

'What?'

Charity saw that by the way he fumbled with his glasses he was far from being in a receptive mood.

'Look, I don't want to talk shop right now,' he went on. 'Apart from a few lectures I've given, I've been out of genetic engineering for a couple of years. If you want another sensational story you'll have to find someone else . . . '

'That stew smells wonderful,' said Charity brightly. 'Shall I dish up?'

After supper Charity decided that she was sitting opposite a very attractive man. Having exhausted his animosity towards her, and relaxed by the Old Oak, he became a friendly and amusing host. He talked of adventures on exotic lands where he had undertaken projects for the World Health Organisation, and about his passion for gliding. Behind his rimless glasses his eyes sparkled as he described his new Blanik sailplane just imported from Czechoslovakia and still crated in a London warehouse.

'You'll have to come with me when I take her up,' he said. 'I'll show you what it felt like to be Icarus, soaring up there in the silence.'

A brass clock ticked away the seconds companionably, and the two people in their little shell of light and warmth on the night water found themselves regarding each other with increasing empathy. And as the level of the rum sank in the bottle, their confidences increased in reverse ratio.

Charity was surprised to find herself lowering her habitual guard as she told him about her adored father who had left the Caribbean to work for London Transport, and her older brother who had become a geologist and now worked for an oil company.

She admitted how hard she had found it to begin her radio career, told him about the offer of a television series and then, changing the subject completely, she was relieved that he did not laugh when she explained that she had lived a previous life in ancient Egypt.

Paul, ignoring the coldly scientific side of his nature, felt he could almost believe her. In the subdued light her skin was dark gold like the mask of some princess in a burial chamber in the Valley of the Queens. And as she spoke with her customary animation it was like watching such a mask come to life.

With the old grievance evaporated, he felt as though he was meeting her for the first time, and with it came an almost overwhelming surge of physical attraction.

Around midnight, when she was sure that there was no danger of his antagonism reviving, she launched into the story about the young man at Eyam and the D-Notice sent to Radio City.

'Imagine what it would mean if the Black Death returned to London,' she said earnestly. But it was obvious Paul's thoughts were far from the idea of such a catastrophe as he leaned comfortably against the upholstery.

'You haven't been listening,' she accused.

'I have,' he lied with a smile. 'Heard every word you said.'

Opening his eyes, he removed his glasses with slow deliberation and leaned across the table to regard Charity as though she was some new fascinating specimen in his laboratory.

'Please,' she said almost desperately, 'I need your help . . . '

'And I think I need yours,' he answered.

Quite unexpectedly his arms were round her, drawing her towards him. Next moment Charity felt his breath on her cheek, then his lips hard on hers, and she found no difficulty in responding.

'Baron Frankenstein!'

To Paul, prone under a tangle of blankets on the starboard bunk, the words seemed to reach him from a tremendous distance. At their sound he began to float towards wakefulness through a sea of pleasurable sensation. He was aware of extreme bodily well-being, a gentle rocking reminding him that he had been sleeping on his boat. But during the night he had not been alone . . .

His mind filled with hot and erotic memory, memory of lamplight on a dark skin and of a warm smile that had floated before him until it had briefly dissolved into an expression of pure ecstasy, just as his own body had sung in its every fibre. And before soft night enveloped him, there was memory of warm limbs peacefully entwined with his, of intimate endearment whispered in his ear.

Now he moved his hand, hoping to feel warm flesh and prove it had not been an extraordinary dream – a nocturnal visit from a beautiful succubus – but his fingers only slid across fabric until they reached the edge of the bunk.

'Baron Frankenstein!'

He forced his eyelids open and saw speckles of cold sunlight on the cabin ceiling reflected from the rippling water outside.

Carefully elevating his head he saw Charity, her trenchcoat over her shoulders as a token dressing gown, holding out a mug of fragrant coffee towards him. The combination of her fresh smiling face beneath her tousled hair brought him back to reality, and he heard himself apologising for having drunk too much the night before and . . .

'Please don't spoil anything with apologies,' said Charity. 'We had a lovely evening which I probably remember better than you because you were already ahead on drinks when I reached *Blue Flame* yesterday.'

'But I was so bloody rude when you turned up.'

'You made up for it, darling,' she laughed. 'What you need is some breakfast and then I've got to get my message across to you . . . '

'Tell me one thing,' he said, raising himself up on his elbow. 'Are you free, or was this a one-night stand?'

'I'm not committed to anyone, if that's what you mean,' Charity answered. 'And last night you explained at great length that your ivory-tower life-style hasn't exactly encouraged lasting relationships, so there we are. Shall we give it time to see what develops?'

He nodded solemnly.

'Now tell me where I'll find the bacon and eggs.'

An hour later, shaved and tidy but still a little pale, Paul cast off the mooring lines while the cruiser's Seawolf engine idled throatily and a column of steam rose from the exhaust. In a borrowed sweater and donkey jacket, Charity sat on the stern seat and watched Paul's activity with an approving look. There was a deftness and a decision about his movements which pleased her. She sincerely hoped that her night on *Blue Flame* would be the prelude to a deeper knowledge of the man who hid behind the image of a mildly eccentric and untidy professor.

Following the night's rain, the sky had a washed look and bare trees edged the horizon like fine lace. Cold sunlight flashed on patches of hoar-frost and transformed the canal into a blue mirror on which two swans cut silent ripples.

'I see now that winter cruising can have a certain charm,' she admitted.

'It's having the place all to myself that I like,' Paul responded as he pushed the bow away from the reed-fringed bank and then leapt aboard. 'Perhaps I'm anti-social, but I do like to get away from it all.'

Standing on the helmsman's platform he pushed the gear lever into the forward position with a practised movement of his knee. As the cruiser surged ahead he spun the wheel and kicked the lever into reverse so that the craft began turning within her own length. Just as the stern was about to hit the bank, he put the lever once more into forward, the bows swung into the centre of the narrow channel and they were gliding down the stretch of the Grand Union known as Fenny Pound.

'Neat,' approved Charity.

'Trying to impress you,' he admitted. 'To be serious. If you really believe there's a bubonic plague outbreak being hushed up, the only way to break a bureaucratic clamp-down is by producing evidence.'

She nodded.

'It seems to me our best chance to get a specimen is in the next few hours before the corpse is – er – specially disposed of. When that woman rang you, did she give you the name of the hospital where her husband died?'

'She said that she was ringing from St John's Fever Hospital. She was told that he'd died from Super flu but she couldn't see his body and she would have to stay in quarantine.'

Paul nodded as he steered *Blue Flame* under a low bridge, its bricks still grooved by ropes with which horses had once towed narrow boats.

'I did a lab course there in my younger days,' Paul said. 'With luck I may still be able to find my way to the morgue.'

5

. . . and among the news topics we'll be discussing here on Radio City are NASA's successful shuttle orbit of the moon, BA's first Concorde flight to Moscow, and the East Germans' official invitation for an international team of experts to investigate Volkstadt. At home, Oxford Street stores report a record spending spree and the leader of the Social Democrats denies rumours of a Lib-So Dem rift . . .

In the chilly over-lit mortuary Gordon the Ghoul – as the gross attendant was known by the staff of St John's Fever Hospital – whistled an endless single note as he cleaned up after an autopsy. When his stainless steel pails were sterilised he'd be able to retire to his little office for a cup of cocoa and a listen to Radio City's late-night phone-in.

He paused as a tall figure, masked like himself and wearing a green lab coat, walked in with a small case.

'I'm from path,' he announced. 'We need a specimen from Delgardo.'

'New, ain't you? You want the customer in Number 12.'

The Ghoul waddled to where the dead lay in tiers of refrigerated cabinets. 'Down for special disposal,' he added, sliding out a long, frosted drawer. 'I'm expecting the meat waggon any minute.'

Dressed in a shroud soaked with antiseptic and sealed in a clear plastic body bag, Leroy Delgardo stared blankly into the radiance flooding from the ceiling.

'Bit late for specimens, ain't it,' muttered Gordon suspiciously. 'I mean, him sealed up an' all. He's booked for night cremation and you know what that means.'

'There was a little accident in the lab,' Paul explained. 'A specimen got incinerated by mistake. If the director finds out it could mean someone's job. I'm just trying to put things right. No need to unseal him, I only need a few ccs of fluid.'

He took a fold of notes out of his gown pocket and slipped them to the attendant.

'Okay, go ahead quick as you can. I'm just going to have me cocoa. I'll get you to sign the usual chitty before you leave.'

Paul ran his hand over the plastic-covered corpse until his fingers located a hard swelling in the groin, then took a hypodermic syringe from his bag. He inserted the long needle through the plastic into the bubo, then carefully drew back the plunger. He gave a grunt of relief as he saw the glass barrel fill with opaque fluid.

He placed the syringe in a special container, pushed the drawer back and a moment later was hurrying down a deserted basement corridor, breathing deeply to rid his lungs of the reek of formaldehyde.

As he climbed into Charity's car in the hospital car-park, Gordon the Ghoul returned to his silent domain.

'Bloody 'ell,' he muttered as he saw that the room was deserted. He went over to the drawer with Number 12 stencilled on it and breathed a sigh of relief when he saw its occupant was intact. He sensed that something irregular had taken place, but as the undertaker's van would soon remove the evidence he need not worry. Besides, the stranger's money would be handy for Christmas.

'Get what you went after?' asked Charity as she put the Mercedes into forward drive.

'I managed to extract some edema fluid,' Paul said. 'Once we get to the lab we'll know the answer pretty soon.'

Charity drove swiftly until she reached Bloomsbury where, at Paul's direction, she turned out of Cartwright Gardens into a street of neglected Regency houses with sad neon scribbles behind their windows advertising vacancies.

'Pull up over here, please,' he said, pointing to a nondescript building with a sign over its shabby entrance which read 'Coram Institute of Biology'.

'You can go home now. I'll ring you in the morning with

the result,' he said.

'No way. I'm seeing this through.'

Paul unlocked the door and, seeing Charity's puzzled look, explained, 'It's really a commercial lab I have a financial share in. We do work for companies without their own facilities, and sometimes I find it useful for my own experimental work since – ah – since my state grant was cut.'

They entered a long room which reminded Charity of her old school laboratory complete with balances in glass cases, Bunsen burners, tangles of glass tubing and some racks of battered-looking electronic equipment and oscilloscopes.

Paul grinned as he noticed her sceptical expression.

'You'd be surprised at what gets done here with test tube and pipette. While I set up, could you hunt out a World Health Organisation bulletin containing *Recommended Laboratory Methods for the Diagnosis of Plague.* I think you'll find it in volume fourteen. I'm afraid I'm a bit rusty on bacilli identification.'

While Charity's gaze roved along lines of books behind tall glass-fronted bookcases Paul produced a sealed box of sterile slides and began to gown up in protective paper overalls which he would incinerate immediately after the tests.

When Charity brought him the required publication he studied several pages with professional intensity in the light of a desk lamp.

'Okay,' he said at length. 'I'll take a look at our little friends in the sterile cubicle.'

He opened the air-tight door of a glass-panelled booth in which a microscope with a camera attachment was mounted on a small metal bench.

'All I can say is that I hope I find you're mistaken,' he muttered as his gloved hands adjusted the special mask over his face.

When the door was sealed behind him he squirted the contents of his syringe into a small flask, then with a slim glass rod transferred a drop of the fluid on to a glass slide and swiftly sealed the container. With another rod he introduced a drop of dye on to his specimen after which he mounted a second slide over the first and sealed the edges with sterile tape.

The slide was clipped beneath the microscope's objective lens, a bright light shone through the condenser and Paul leaned over the binocular eyepieces. For a long minute he adjusted the controls, then turned to the glass window.

'Slip on a gown and mask and bring me the bulletin,' he mouthed. 'I need to compare the bacilli I've got with the illustrations.'

Charity put on overalls, gloves and mask and opened the door of the sterile cubicle.

'Here, Paul,' she said, laying the open bulletin on the bench beside him. As she did so its corner touched the fragile flask, tipping it over the edge.

The noise as it broke on the ceramic floor was no more than a tinkle, but to Paul it was like an explosion. With the savage movement of his arm he sent Charity reeling out of the cubicle and slammed the door shut. Standing in the corner of the confined cubicle, he gazed sick-faced at the puddle of liquid in which the shards of glass reflected fluorescent light.

'Please God it's non-virulent,' he whispered. For a moment he looked about helplessly, then saw a row of glass-topped bottles on a rack beyond the microscope and picked up one labelled C2H5OH. Quickly he poured some solvent over the yellowish fluid. Taking a book of matches from his pocket, he struck one and threw it on to the alcohol which gushed into pale fire.

Outside the cubicle he said, 'Sorry I was so rough, but that little splash could have been one of the most concentrated forms of known death. Don't come near me until I've finished and put this clothing into the furnace.'

When the flame died he re-entered the cubicle and looked at the open page of the bulletin, then into the eye-pieces. He touched the focussing wheel delicately, and with a sigh stood back.

'I'm ninety-nine per cent sure it's *Pasteurella pestis,*' he said.

The streets were filling with early morning workers when

Paul and Charity entered a small café close to the Russell Square Underground station. While waiting for coffee they scanned the armful of newspapers they had bought from the vendor outside.

'Not a word about plague in any of them, just stories about Super flu,' said Paul. 'Yet the authorities have known longer than you and I what that man Delgardo died of.'

'I told you there's a conspiracy of silence,' said Charity.

'The public must be warned. Handled the right way a vaccination programme could be started and panic avoided, though serum would have to be brought in from all over the world. But how the hell can we raise the alarm if there's an official news black-out?'

'We'll go and see The Digger. I've got him the story of a lifetime.'

In his sleek office Vic Kelly lounged behind his desk, sucking at a cigar as though it were rather unpleasant.

Charity leaned forward in her chair as she tried to impress him with the urgency of her words.

' . . . So I persuaded Paul – Dr Mitchell – to help me get proof that the Black Death has returned . . . '

'He's the fair-haired streak I saw waiting in reception?' asked Vic. 'You must have worked a miracle to get his co-operation after your last beat-up on him.'

'As a medical man and a biologist, he saw the seriousness of the situation,' Charity said primly, and described how she had driven him at midnight to St John's Fever Hospital.

'Sounds a bit Burke and Hare,' said Vic, stubbing out his half-smoked cigar. 'So he's got proof that the plague bugs are rampaging in London.'

She nodded.

'We have microscopic photographs of the bacilli and a sealed specimen. I can go on the air at any minute and blow the story wide open.'

'Sure you can.' Vic frowned and took another cigar from an oval tin. 'What the hell do I want this for?' he growled to himself and put it back. 'Let's have a drink, girl, we're both going to need one.' He stalked across his white carpet to the drinks cabinet.

'The usual? I have to tell you, Charity, there'll be no plague story – at least not until there's an official announcement.'

She gaped at him.

'But . . . '

'Listen, while you were off hunting Frankenstein up the Grand Union, I – along with what might be laughingly referred to as the responsible representatives of the pommy media – was invited to County Hall. Peter Barnet gave us an explanation of the D-Notices, and it was agreed to respect them. So, sorry kid, but no story.'

'You mean, you're letting yourself be muzzled by a health official who wants to get his department off the hook,' Charity cried. 'You're passing up a story like this, perhaps the story of a century . . . '

He nodded.

'And you're the man who advised me when I joined Radio City never to drink blood through a straw! What's happened to the Anzac spirit, Vic?'

He returned to his desk, a large Bells in his hand in place of the usual Fosters.

'It isn't all that straight-bloody-forward,' he said slowly. 'You know I had the hots for this story, but, when you're in my job, other considerations crop up – like loyalty to one's shareholders. It was put to me that if I disregarded the D-Notice, Radio City's broadcasting licence would be unfavourably reviewed. Get the picture? And I'll tell you something for nothing – they weren't kidding! There won't be a peep out of the media about this business until it's either blown over – or got out of hand.'

'But they can't hold back a story as big as this . . .'

'Why not? It happened over the abdication in the thirties. And maybe they're right. So far there has been only a tiny outbreak but news of it could start an exodus from London. And think how our advertisers would react to such a story just as Christmas shopping is getting under way.'

'People have a right to know what threatens them.'

'Don't go bloody pompous on me!'

'I'll get my story out somehow.'

'Not on Radio City you won't.'

'Radio City isn't the only outlet.'

'Listen, Charity, I know how you must feel. It couldn't have been fun for you having to swallow your pride and make peace with that kookie professor, or help him raid the morgue, but skip being the ace radio journalist for a minute. As far as you're concerned there are bigger issues at stake. I can tell you unofficially that you'll be elected to the board if . . . '

'If?' asked Charity suspiciously.

'If you don't play the drongo over this story. We couldn't afford to have a board member stirring up a nation-wide panic. And as a board member you've got to realise that such a story won't bring in an extra penny of revenue . . . '

'Vic, they've really got at you.'

'They fair dinkum have,' he agreed gloomily.

In reception Paul started to his feet as Charity appeared, surprised at the dangerous gleam in her normally doe-like eyes.

'Dr Mitchell, you can take me to lunch,' she declared.

As they strode up Fleet Street into a bitter wind, Charity finished her tirade against The Digger and said, 'There's still a way of breaking the story – you're going to be on the *Guest Host* telly show.'

'Yeah, well . . . like I said . . . I used to do a bit of strippin' before I made it into the music business,' the girl with the tangerine coloured hair told Charity as they faced each other in a pool of hot light. 'So it seemed natural-like to build it into the act.' She gave her famous *gamin* grin. 'I don't know which it was that got me into the charts, me voice or me vulva . . . '

The greying producer behind the console desk in studio B control room said wearily, 'Camera 3!'

Obediently the finger of his pretty production assistant pressed an illuminated key and the frame surrounding the screen monitoring Camera 3 glowed green. Beneath similar rack-mounted sets was a sound-proofed window giving the production team a view of the studio where Charity, elegant on a high stool, was interviewing Mandy

Devine, lead singer of The Strippers which had just been voted the top pop group of the year.

'Camera 2, close up on the bitch,' the producer murmured into his microphone.

The image on the second monitor screen flickered, then steadied as the camera zoomed in.

'Okay, Camera 2 – now!'

The PA pressed the appropriate key and the frame of light jumped to the screen filled with Mandy's face.

The producer flipped a switch so that his voice buzzed in the earphones of the floor manager hovering just out of camera range.

'Eddie, sixty seconds to go on this one and then the Prof makes his entrance . . . Camera 3, line up on the arch.'

On the studio floor a camera swung away from the two young women and its operator focussed on the property doorway through which Paul Mitchell was about to be prodded.

'All righty, Camera 1 on. Camera 2, I want you to freeze on the Prof's face when Charity is doing her spiel, we may get a good reaction shot. Wind 'em up, Eddie.'

The floor manager made a revolving motion with his right hand to warn Charity that time was running out. A sound engineer checked the microphone boom above her head as the lighting was about to change – it must not cast a shadow across her face.

'Finally, Mandy, we're all fascinated to know if you and the other girls enjoy flinging off your clothes at the climax of your concerts,' said Charity.

'Enjoyment isn't the right word,' said the pop star, tossing back her flaming hair. 'By then we're hyped along with the fans and, I mean, you don't think of it like doin' an ordinary strip – it's like a lovely great orgy. It's natural like, and a lot better than taking a chain-saw to your guitar. I mean, there's great identification, a lot of the girls in the audience start rippin' off along with us.'

'Sounds fun. And your next performance is in just a few days?'

'Yeah, Christmas Eve at Wembley. A right sell-out but it may be cold . . . '

'I'm sure you'll keep everybody warm, Mandy, and thanks for coming on the show.'

Charity looked directly at the nearest camera.

'If any of you out there are not sure what The Strippers are all about, here's a clip from their last performance, though we can't show you the explicit full frontal finale . . . sorry.'

'Roll video,' snapped the producer.

Beat music pulsed from the monitors and a line of girls with assorted instruments gyrated on a strobe-lit stage while Mandy, dangerously close to the edge of the platform, threw away her mike and tugged savagely at her shirt. As it tore free her sweat-streaked breasts were greeted with an ecstatic roar from the audience. She swung the shirt round her head like a flag – a red flag of rebellion – then began to unbuckle the cowboy belt of her jeans. Behind her the group discarded their guitars and saxophones and stripped to the frantic rhythm of the drummer, the only male musician in the group and too busy to shed his loin cloth or the tiger skin draped across his shoulders.

'Cut video,' said the producer. 'Camera 1.'

Charity swam into focus on the first monitor screen.

'I guess that beats panto,' she laughed. Serious again she continued, 'And now for our last guest, and I must admit that I'm nervous about meeting him. He and I have crossed swords before. As a result of my radio interview on the dangers of genetic engineering he became known as a modern Frankenstein – a man with the capability of creating horrendous life forms – and his controversial experimental programme was halted. So he has no reason to like me, and I think shows a generous spirit by agreeing to come on the show tonight.'

'Good stuff,' approved the producer. 'Camera 3, Betty.'

The PA activated the camera channel just as Paul Mitchell walked through the plaster archway and casually seated himself on the stool from which Mandy Devine had been hustled during the video clip.

'Welcome, Dr Paul Mitchell,' said Charity solemnly. 'You come in peace, I hope.'

'Miss Brown, how could an old monster-maker like me

remain angry with someone as beautiful as you?'

Charity rewarded him with the warm smile that was perfect for television, a flash of even teeth coupled with a humorous sparkle in her liquid eyes.

'Thank you, doctor. I know that you have not come on to *Guest Host* just to chat. As a microbiologist you have been delving into the past to learn about something which could possibly affect us today.'

'That's right. I've been investigating the Black Death . . . '

'Son-of-a-bitch! Here it comes!' exclaimed the producer who chose oaths suggestive of a transatlantic background. He was aware the door had opened and closed, and two strangers were behind him.

'But surely that's a little out of date?' Charity was saying.

'I wish it were so,' said Paul, looking straight at the camera on which a tiny red light glowed. Although carefully coached by Charity, he found it hard to believe he was addressing millions of people. 'Most of us dismiss the Great Plague of London as something buried away in the history books, but . . . '

'Before you go on, can you tell us something about it.'

'Certainly. The Great Plague began in December, 1664, with the death of two Frenchmen in Long Acre. The family they had boarded with tried to hush up the cause of death, but rumour spread and the Secretaries of State sent two physicians to investigate. As a result it was announced in the weekly bill of mortality that plague had appeared in London which caused the public great concern, though no one had any conception of the horror which lay ahead.

'From those bills of mortality we can trace the growth of the epidemic and how it gradually spread across the city. They tell us that over 70,000 Londoners perished out of 460,000.'

'That's roughly a sixth of the population,' Charity exclaimed.

'Yes, bubonic plague is the most deadly epidemic known to man, but because it has not affected Europe for three centuries it has received little attention in the West. Indeed, the best descriptions of its effect are still to be found in seventeenth century accounts such as Daniel Defoe's *Journal of the Plague Year*.

'Listen to this,' he continued as he unfolded a piece of paper and adjusted his glasses to read. 'Here he tells about people who had become infected without realising it " . . . such as had received the contagion, and had it really upon them, and in their blood, yet did not show the consequences of it in their countenances; nay, even were not sensible of it themselves, as many were not for several days. These breathed death in every place, and upon everybody who came near them; nay, their very clothes retained the infection, their hands would infect the things they touched . . . Now it was impossible to know these people, nor did they sometimes, as I have said, know themselves to be infected. These were the people that so often dropped down and fainted in the streets; for oft-times they would go about the streets to the last, till on a sudden they would sweat, grow faint, sit down at a door and die." '

'That's certainly vivid journalism,' said Charity. 'But what has it to do with us?'

'Back in 1979 Dr Frederick J. Wright, of Edinburgh University, warned the British Association that bubonic plague could return to Britain via air travellers.

'Now that millions of people move around the world each year, the dangers are greatly increased. In the days of sea travel anyone carrying the plague would usually die before the journey was over, but in an aircraft a person newly infected in India could be in England before the symptoms became evident.

'The World Health Organisation and local medical authorities do everything in their power to reduce the risk, but what is not generally realised is that it is not just passengers or crew who might spread the disease, but the very jets in which they fly. Viruses could be transported in the upholstery or in the waste products that have to be off-loaded, or even on the bodies of aircraft during their global loops.'

'So whether it's a result of international air travel – or something like the Volkstadt germ warfare scare – you believe we could be threatened by the Black Death again.'

'It's not that we could be – we are,' Paul declared. 'I have evidence that death has occurred through a new visitation of plague in London, yet the authorities, in full knowledge of this, are hushing the matter up, and blaming the symptoms on so-called Super flu. I do not wish to speculate on their motives – what is more important is that with every hour that passes bacilli are multiplying and we are running out of time.'

He looked earnestly into the cold eye of the camera.

'I'm not saying this to cause a panic. If proper steps are taken immediately there is no need for panic. Today, if plague is diagnosed early, it will respond to antibiotics. But health authorities must act immediately . . . '

'You say you have evidence that people have already died of plague in London,' cut in Charity. 'It seems incredible.'

Paul held up a sealed slide.

'In here I have a specimen of plague bacilli which I personally removed from the body of one of the victims.'

Following a whisper in his earphones, the floor manager began his winding-up signal. The programme was within seconds of its conclusion.

'So what is your message tonight, doctor?'

'There is no doubt that plague is in London, and co-incidentally at exactly the same time of the year and with similar weather conditions in which the Great Plague began. Then the progress across London was slow because people did not travel from one end of the city to another as they do today.

'Now Londoners make two million journeys daily on the Underground, and crowded in over-heated trains they are in the ideal environment for the spread of bacilli, and in these mobile incubators they will carry infection to every corner of the city.

'Until the danger is over people must stay in their homes. The authorities must begin an immediate vaccination programme and there must be a ban on travel unless a certificate of health can be produced. Everyone with the slightest symptom of what appears to be a cold, or who has a feeling of being under the weather, should be put on a course of antibiotics and isolated.'

Paul paused. Behind his professorish spectacles his eyes blazed with sincerity.

'I call upon the government to face up to the fact that we are threatened and take precautions to prevent a catastrophe.'

Charity broke the following silence to ask, 'From what you know of the original cases, when do you think more people will go down with the disease?'

'The usual incubation period for plague is between three and six days. My guess is that in a couple of days there will be such a wave of cases in London it will be impossible to continue the cover-up . . . the Second Great Plague of London will have broken out.'

The floor manager made a chopping motion with his hand, the sound engineer brought up theme music, the producer muttered his ritual 'Thank you, folks,' and unfastened his lapel mike.

As the lights began to fade in the studio the technicians looked curiously at Paul and Charity. Hardly a word was said as cameras were rolled away and cables coiled.

'Well, Paul, we've done it,' breathed Charity. 'Twelve million viewers have got your message.'

'Sorry to disillusion you,' said the producer, approaching grim-faced. 'The show didn't go out live. I had instructions from on high to tape it and a party political broadcast replaced it on the network.'

'You mean . . . nobody saw or heard me outside this studio,' said Paul incredulously.

'That's exactly what I do mean. As for you, Miss Brown, you switched agreed content so that my programme would become a platform to promote yourself through sheer goddamned sensationalism. Think what would have happened to the ratings if a phoney scare story like this had gone out just before Christmas!' He actually shuddered at the thought. 'But one thing I promise you – you'll never set foot in here again. You can keep your two-faced Caribbean charm for steam radio. I don't take kindly to being conned . . .'

He turned on his heel.

Two men, in raincoats despite the air-conditioning, appeared at the door of the studio.

'Who could have tipped them off?' Paul muttered.

'I can guess,' said Charity bitterly.

The strangers approached and Paul and Charity climbed from their stools as one said, 'Dr Paul Mitchell, I am a special branch police officer and I am arresting you for an offence relating to the desecration of a human body. I must warn you . . .'

'Yes, yes,' said Paul. 'I understand.'

'And you, miss,' said the other. 'You must accompany us. As a result of your association with Dr Mitchell it is possible you could be infected with a contagious disease. You will be required to spend some days in restricted quarantine.' For a moment his face lost its professional impassivity. 'It was a good try,' he conceded.

Paul and Charity walked to the exit followed by the two policemen and an impatient electrician killed the studio lights.

6

Phil Jason with the bad news, folks. Our one and only Miss Brown has gone down with the dreaded Super bug, so tonight there will be no Charity Show. I can hear your gasps of dismay right here in the studio! But despair not this Yuletide Eve – in place of Charity I'm taking you live to the last hour of The Strippers' concert at Wembley. How about that, then – Jason to the rescue! And if you need a laugh think on this: the New Britain Party announce they'll be holding a torch-light vigil outside the concert as a protest against national degeneracy . . . they'll need those torches on a freezer like this . . . Beep! Beep!

Charity opened her eyes and felt a scream form in her throat – the head of the white creature gazing down at her was cylindrical, had large goggle-like eyes but was without nostrils or mouth.

'There's no need for alarm,' assured a muffled voice.

The girl half rose on her bed and gazed around for escape. She was in a small windowless room which – like the creature approaching her – was completely white.

'I know I look like a space alien,' the voice continued. 'But under this prophylactic suit I'm a very ordinary human being.' He chuckled in a way that suggested that while he might be a human he was far from ordinary, and sat on a metal hospital chair.

'What . . . what am I doing here?' Charity asked, still bewildered by her colourless surroundings and her strange bed. 'I can't focus . . . have I been in an accident?'

'What you're feeling is the effect of a strong tranquilliser we gave you along with a shot of antibiotics when you were brought in. You've been asleep for quite a long time.'

The figure chuckled again as though it were rather a joke.

Layer by layer the drug-induced mist cleared from her memory. She remembered sitting in the hot studio with Paul Mitchell, of being escorted out by strangers and rushed through the night in some sort of van or ambulance to a Victorian building looming in shadowy grounds. Here she was separated from Paul and hustled into this room where, despite her protests, a silver needle was eased into a vein in her left arm.

'You've kidnapped me,' she accused, bolt upright in her indignation. 'Where the hell am I – and where's Dr Mitchell?'

'Young lady, don't excite yourself,' soothed the mummy-like figure. 'Everything has been for your own good, even though you appear to have been rather naughty.'

Charity relaxed against the pillows. The exertion had caused a painful drumbeat in her head.

'Okay – so why have I been naughty? Are you a member of the Thought Police?'

'Not exactly,' replied the voice with irritating good

humour, 'but in this complex age certain arms of the administration do have to maintain – shall we say – *security* aspects of which the public is of necessity unaware.'

'So Orwell wasn't far out!'

Laughter came from behind the blank mask.

'Oh dear, you journalists do love melodrama. And I'm afraid it is your penchant for the melodramatic which has brought you here. Really, that scare story you tried to put out . . . '

'But there has been death from plague in London.'

The white head shook from side to side.

'Dr Mitchell identified the bacilli . . . '

'Miss Brown, that slide, which your friend waved in front of the camera as so-called evidence, was found to contain nothing more than a spot of dye used for staining microscopic specimens.'

'Then if there's no plague why am I a prisoner?'

'You're not a prisoner, Miss Brown. You're not under arrest, you're here for your own good. You see, your misguided friend did have contact with a cadaver which had died from an infectious disease, and as a result he could have become contagious and in turn infected you. We will keep you here until we are sure that you are free from anything nasty. Your absence from work has been put down to indisposition so you have no problem there. In a few days you can return to normal life.'

The figure rose.

'And what about Paul?'

'Ah yes, the tarnished Dr Mitchell. Well, he has broken the law by violating a dead body. The police may decide to lay charges once his period of quarantine is over.

'If you feel hungry or want some magazines to read, press that button and a nurse in similar attire will come. Make the most of your little holiday and, may I suggest, when it is over forget the whole episode . . . if you don't want to be arrested for aiding and abetting Dr Mitchell. As there has been no outbreak of plague it would be obvious to the public that you were prepared to cruelly hoax them for the sake of sensationalism, and I am sure you can appreciate the effect of that on your career.'

'Tell me, please, who are you?'

But the figure made no reply as it approached the door which opened briefly as if someone outside had been observing through a spyhole, then closed again with the soft click of a well-oiled lock.

Charity's head still ached and she felt lethargic from whatever it was they had fed into her bloodstream. She was not sure whether it was this sense of weakness which brought tears close to her eyes, or the fear that she had allowed herself to be mistaken all along.

My guess is that in a couple of days there will be such a wave of cases in London it will be impossible to continue the cover-up . . . the Second Great Plague of London will have broken out.

'I thought Mitchell's remarks might be of interest to you,' said the Permanent Under-Secretary of Health as he switched off the video set in Peter Barnet's office. He turned to the window for a panoramic view of the Thames. 'The fellow must have a chip on his shoulder because his genetic engineering programme was suspended. And as for that Brown woman, she's obviously anti-authority like all . . . '

'I'm sure they acted sincerely,' Peter Barnet said. His eyes were red-rimmed and he leaned wearily on his desk. 'We could have had an appalling situation on our hands. I haven't been able to sleep thinking about it. Just imagine . . . '

'At my age I've been through too many potential crises to lose sleep,' the Under-Secretary said, watching a tug with a string of barges speeding on the down-river tide. 'We live on endless knife edges these days only, thank the Lord, the public rarely realises it. This little panic is just one more blade. Next week it could be a train smash with a cargo of waste for Windscale . . .'

'Yes, but in this case we knew of the possibility in advance. We are accountable.'

The Under-Secretary gestured to a huge wall map of London, parts of which were forested with multi-coloured pins, and said, 'At least there have been no new cases.'

'No, all the men who entered the plague pit are dead apart from one named Hacker who's vanished. He'd given the contracting company a false address, to dodge tax I suppose. We've done everything possible to discreetly isolate those who had contact with the deceased and treat them with massive doses of antibiotics before any *Pasteurella pestis* bacilli could develop. And it could be – pray God – that the infection caught by the building site workers was only virulent enough to affect them.

'Our only other case is the man from Pinner and as he's still in a coma we haven't been able to trace how he got it. If we can get through another couple of days without a new case we can write it off as a freak outbreak and your precious Minister and his colleagues needn't worry in case Volkstadt is blamed.'

The Under-Secretary turned back into the room.

'And the authorities of this great city will not be blamed for the plague pit situation. Incidentally, what do you intend to do about the plague pits?'

'In due course every known pit will be traced and covered with cement in the same way they seal off nuclear spoil.'

'It's not the first time that a little scare like this has taken place,' mused the Under-Secretary. 'There was quite an odd happening during the Great Paris Exhibition. An American girl went out for a day's sight-seeing, leaving her mother, who was off-colour after the voyage, resting in their hotel room. When she returned in the evening she went up to the room, which was at the end of the corridor, only to find a blank wall.

'She went down to the reception desk where the manager professed he had never seen her before.

'You can imagine the effect of such a bizarre situation on a young woman, especially as she could not speak French. Had she come into the wrong hotel by mistake? It certainly looked familiar enough! Then she had an idea. She opened the guest register and was about to point to where she and her mother had signed in when she saw there was another name on the line.

'She became hysterical, the gendarmes came and the

staff – who had served the girl and her mother that morning – swore that they did not know her. She was taken to hospital as an amnesia case where she remained until she was fit to return home.

'What had actually happened was that during the girl's outing the mother had collapsed with cholera and the authorities, fearing the effect such news would have on the thousands of visitors who had flocked to the city, had arranged an elaborate if somewhat macabre cover-up.'

The Under-secretary laughed but Peter Barnet frowned at the big map with its pins, each representing a plague suspect who had been checked out under the pretence of Super flu.

Thank God those who had used the emergency telephone numbers were either hypochondriacs or really were suffering with bad bouts of flu. But he was still prey to complex pangs of guilt, and he had hated the Paris story. He had been party to a similar – if less dramatic – deception and at this moment two people were being held against their will because they knew the truth.

On the other hand, suppose the Paul Mitchell interview had gone out. The resultant panic might have been more dangerous than the ancient virus which had only claimed those whose greed had led them into the pit. He must get a grip on himself, especially in front of the sardonic civil servant.

'I must be getting back,' said the Under-Secretary. 'The Cabinet is expecting an advance report from the WHO team which the East Germans invited to Volkstadt . . . '

He was interrupted by the buzz of an internal phone on the Chief Medical Officer's desk. He noticed that Peter Barnet's face twitched slightly as he picked up the receiver and held it to his ear, but he was not prepared for the expression of horror which followed it.

The half-mile-long supertanker *Amocolavery* ploughed through the leaden Atlantic swell en route for Savannah with its tanks full of North Sea crude. Hunched over the taffrail, Hacker watched an albatross glide effortlessly along the wake which stretched like a foaming highway to the horizon. With his hands in the pockets of his donkey jacket, and his long hair whipped about his face by the cruel wind, he savoured his solitude.

His off-duty mates were in the comfortable crew's lounge watching a video of *Swedish Sex Kittens*, but he preferred to be alone with his thoughts. Several days ago he had paid his bribe to work his passage to the United States. Now, as he flicked his cigarette butt past the ensign staff, he congratulated himself yet again on having got out of England after hearing that several men who had entered the pit with him had been taken ill. For a while he had been scared of developing symptoms, but now enough time had elapsed for him to be sure that he had escaped the ancient infection.

Under his dungarees there was the pleasant feel of a body belt. In it were stitched the gold coins which, once he was in the States, would give him a taste of the life for which he had always hungered. First of all he'd buy a car – a big powerful American car – to carry him to the sun belt, to sun-kissed girls and sun-drenched freedom.

His winter of discontent was over.

'Oi, I tell you it is something I do not like,' old Mrs Polanski said. 'On the landing the smell is so bad.'

'Look, Mum, if there are bad smells around you call a plumber or the gas board but not the police,' said the young constable. 'The last time you called me round here was because you thought spies had bugged your bedroom.'

'Spies – what spies?' cried Mrs Polanski. 'I have nothing to do with spies. Why you say "spies"?'

The constable sighed.

'Sorry, I must have been mistaken,' he said. 'Now you have a blocked drain . . . right?'

'Blocked drain, pouf! You think I call the polezi for a drain? You think I'm crazy in the head? The smell on the landing is no drain, I tell you. Oi, I know that smell. I know it before, in Warsaw when we rose against the Nazis and the heroic Red Army held back until we had been crushed . . .'

'All right, all right, let's go up and take a sniff,' said the constable, remembering it was Christmas Eve. What sort of Christmas would the old girl have alone with her memories of a world that had ended before he'd been born?

He followed her up the creaking stairs to a small landing covered with curling linoleum squares.

'It does pong a bit,' he agreed, taking out his handkerchief. 'How come the other tenants haven't complained?'

'The top flat have gone to spend the Christmas with their parents. And I do not know what has happened to the ones in this flat. I not seen 'Acker, maybe he leave his wife, maybe she leave him. Maybe they both dead in there.'

'Perhaps the spies got them,' muttered the constable, rattling the door.

'I'm not supposed to do this but if it'll put your mind at rest, Mum,' he said, taking a Barclaycard from his wallet. A moment later the flexible plastic pressed back the tongue of the cheap lock and the door swung inwards.

Mrs Polanski wailed to her parthenon of saints as the effluvium of death enveloped them.

The constable remained at the door, hands over his mouth, fighting the spasms which gripped his stomach, trying not to breathe, trying not to cry out.

Old curtains were drawn across the window of the living room of the small flat, but light shone from an electric bulb which must have been burning for days. Directly beneath it lay something that the constable would never quite forget.

For an instant it reminded him of the inflated animal skins which natives somewhere or other used as primitive river rafts. Twice the size of the human body it had once been, the torso was bloated to an extraordinary degree with the belly ballooned as with a monstrous pregnancy and the limbs forced apart by their own obscene swelling. The skin was black except where pressure had caused it to split and reveal grey flesh. Patches of liquid putrefaction seeped from beneath it. As the policeman remained staring, the carcass moved slightly and sighed as the flatus of decomposition gave it a brief and ghastly parody of life. The fluffy curls about the head were the only indication that these were the mortal remains of the Rose of Flowerland.

*

Lancelot Storm – who had changed his name by deed poll from Albert Sugden – felt a glow of pride, which neutralised the occasional snowflakes, as he looked along the members of the Eagle Commando standing like perfectly spaced statues in the gutter facing the entrance to the Wembley Arena. The expression of each was impassive yet made stern by the ruddy light of the torches – hired from the Spotlight Cine Props Company – held at arms' length. If only the law did not prohibit uniforms! They got as near to it as legally possible, each man wearing a white shirt and black tie beneath a neutral anorak, dark trousers and lace-up field boots. And above the heart of each shone the chromed NBP badge.

Opposite the long line of 'super-troopers' stood ranks of equally impassive policemen to keep the peace should the Anti-Fascist League turn up in force. So far the only reaction had been abuse shouted over the shoulders of the police by the stream of fans flowing in to the pop concert.

To Storm the taunts were music. Long ago in Bavaria the same taunts had been flung at the small dedicated group which had met in bierkellers, but before long those taunts had changed to 'heils'. So it would be here. He was convinced that once the aims of the NBP became understood, when the personality of the Leader caught the public imagination, when people had to choose between an extreme socialist society and national freedom, the NBP would be recognised for its historical role. That day would soon be at hand. Now that once-Great Britain was about to ally herself with East Europe, her Aryan people would be shocked out of the apathy which had dogged them since the tragedy of the Second World War.

Storm had waited a long time for The Day.

As he marched along his rigid line of torch-bearers his mind flicked back to that glorious Sunday at the beginning of the sixties when London saw the nearest thing to a Nuremberg rally in Trafalgar Square. Complete with banners and roaring loudspeakers which filled the square with sieg-heils recorded from an earlier era, the speaker called upon all that was best and manly in the Anglo-Saxon heart.

Above him, high on the plinth of Nelson's Column and steady as a figure carved in granite, the standard-bearer held high the national flag from its T-shaped pole.

Albert Sugden, then a teenager whose main preoccupation had been skiffle and a second-hand AJS, was suddenly awakened by the power and the glory of the scene. Even though it had finally broken up in chaos when alien Communists pulled the plugs on the speakers, the picture of that afternoon had remained with him down the years – twenty-five years to be exact. He was no longer young and had suffered his disappointments. He had joined the party immediately after the rally, but then it had been dogged with internal dissension, personality clashes, breakaway groups and a bewildering lack of support by those threatened by the brown tide of immigration. But through it all he had remained loyal to the ideal, and this is what the Leader now recognised. This was why he was in charge of this elite commando on this night of the year when TV cameras would show to the rest of the country how serious, law-abiding and determined the NBP was – not like the caricatures portrayed by the Zion-allied Press.

'Chin higher,' he said as he came to the end of the line where the young standard-bearer gripped a pole which, below an NBP emblem, held a placard proclaiming in Gothic-style script 'Depravity saps the Nation'. Later, when the cameras would be on them, the placard would be replaced by the Union flag.

'Yes, Lance,' said the standard-bearer, correct titles of necessity being forbidden outside the rented Gospel halls where the groups met for physical drill and the weekly taped message from the Leader.

'Good man,' approved Lancelot Storm. The bearer was hardly more than a boy, yet he was tall, innocent-faced and with blond Nordic hair blown attractively across his brow by the gusts of snow-flaked wind.

For a moment their blue eyes met, and then Lance turned abruptly away and walked back along the unflinching line, a tear of pure joy coursing down his frozen cheek.

*

The first half had ended and the capacity audience, despite the efforts of the warm-up group was still restless. It was The Strippers they had come for, and they would not be satisfied until the spotlight cut through the smoky atmosphere and revealed Mandy Devine, ready to blast off with the smash hit 'Lady Santa'.

In the dressing room the group made last minute preparations. The drummer huddled in a duffel coat, swallowed some pills and flexed his cold fingers. Mandy came over to him and asked, 'Got anything to hype me, Rocco? I feel like death. Must be getting this bloody Super flu. For two pins I'd call it off . . . '

At the last three words the manager materialised beside her.

'Do I hear you right? You want to call it off? Know how many fans there are out there waiting for you? Maybe you like suicide, but what about the rest of the group? What about *me*?'

Mandy sighed wearily.

'I just been feelin' bad the last couple of days,' she said. 'I ache all over, reckon I've a temperature and my tongue is too big for my mouth. Just give me something to get me through the next couple of hours, will you?'

'I'll call the doctor,' said the manager. 'He'll give you a shot and then you can rest up over Christmas before we go Stateside, okay?'

'Forget the doctor,' said the drummer. 'Take these, Mandy, they'll hit the spot.'

'You're the expert,' she said with a wan smile as she swallowed the capsules he gave her. 'All right, kids, let's give those freaks out there their money's worth.'

'That's my girl,' approved the manager. 'They've started the fog, better get going . . . '

Out on the stage thin shafts of restlessly changing colour pierced the dry ice cloud materialising on the stage accompanied by wild, rippling chords from a grossly amplified synthesiser.

High in a glass broadcaster's booth, a slender young man with wild hair and sleepy eyes began whispering into his microphone.

'This is your ever-loving Radio City bringing you live – and, boy! do I mean *live!* – The Strippers' Christmas concert from Wembley, where else?' said Phil Jason. 'Not since the magic days of the Beatles and the Stones has a group generated such happy hysteria, and tonight we are going to let you hear the music while I try and tell you what's going on – if my powers of description live up to it.

'When I arrived here tonight I passed a line of gentlemen holding torches in a silent protest against tonight's entertainment – I suppose their idea of fun is hunt the jack-boot . . .'

His patter was interrupted by an explosion of welcome from the audience as The Strippers appeared through the mist like so many Draculas. Mandy Devine stood white-faced in the spotlights until the shouting began to fade, then she struck a jarring note from her electronic guitar and the group burst into the rolling beat against which she chanted 'Lady Santa', which one critic had described as 'the best reason for censorship since the attack on Pearl Harbour'.

On the stage Mandy performed as though possessed. Despite the pain in her body, her mind was strangely excited, and she forced herself to dance, leap and rock in a way that Phil Jason, stunned by her performance, could only tell his audience was 'daemonic'.

'She's not of this world,' he said in an awestruck voice when one number came to an end with Mandy spread-eagled on the floor. 'The Who used to go crazy on stage, but this is unbelievable. The rest of the girls have caught the frenzy – they're giving the performance of their lives. A couple of them are lifting Mandy to her feet . . . she's staggering and . . . she's fallen! She's like a boxer going down for the count . . . it's unbelievable. She's up on her knees now, and shaking her head. You could hear a pin drop in the auditorium. Is there something wrong, or is Mandy up to her old tricks and kidding around with the audience?

'She's kidding! She's back on her feet, and she's doing that funny jump of hers, and as you can hear the group is going into its 'Flashette' number. She sure had us fooled then, she looked like she'd blown her circuits.

'And you can feel the vibes of the audience. Already several have been carried out cold, and now some of the girls are starting to send their buttons flying. I'll belt up now so you can hear . . . '

He switched off the microphone and his sound engineer brought up the music.

From the wings the manager could not take his eyes off the posturing figure of Mandy. He had never seen her so manic. Whatever it was the drummer had slipped her had done the trick. A few more shows like this and he'd have the top group in the world, but this thought could not relieve him of a vague feeling of apprehension. Things had never gone so right at a performance, yet some instinct warned him of danger. Perhaps when the strip came the fans might go berserk – not just a nice little publicity-orientated riot, but a real blood-letting rampage. He hastily looked around for the nearest emergency exit, and he noticed that his tension was shared by the strategically placed stewards unconsciously flexing themselves for the worst.

On stage the penultimate number ended with Mandy on her knees.

An uneasy silence fell, punctuated by cries of fans so carried away that the music still pounded in their brains.

'Okay,' Mandy gasped into her microphone. 'Now we come to what you all come for – and all I can say is I hope that you keep coming . . . an' a Merry Christmas to one an' all!'

She gave her usual grin, but to Phil Jason high in his box it seemed oddly lop-sided. It wouldn't surprise him if the drug squad was waiting in the wings!

Slowly the girl climbed to her feet. By now she was hardly aware of the thousands of fans beyond the halo of light enveloping her and the girls. Her mouth was as dry as paper, her throat a funnel of fire, and her heart was pumping as though she had just run a race.

Her face became a rictus of agony, but it was unnoticed as the strobe lights began to flicker and the fans gave voice. Many were swaying towards the stage, a naked girl climbed on the shoulders of her boyfriend before they toppled in the crush. Following the tradition of earlier concerts, sweaters were thrown into the air and Phil Jason's words tumbled over each other as he tried to describe the scene.

Mandy took her usual place right on the edge of the stage, screaming into the microphone while behind her the rest of the group formed a dancing line.

As the strobes flashed on and off with the cruel brilliance of photographers' flashguns, the delirium of the group seemed to flow over the audience. Scores of youngsters had discarded their clothing and were leaping up and down or spinning like pale-skinned dervishes.

The roar of the crowd doubled. Mandy had flung away her mike and the ritual striptease began.

'Mandy Devine has taken entertainment into a new dimension,' Phil Jason was shouting into his mike. 'She's not a performer to these fans – she's a goddess! And there, she's naked and . . . My God!'

Rocco faltered on the beat as Mandy stood transfixed in the special high-powered spotlight which replaced the strobes. The hurricane-like roar of the crowd began to die. The Strippers in various stages of undress began to cower away from their lead singer. Somewhere someone began to scream.

Mandy's body was like that of a corpse. The whiteness of her thighs was almost obscured by evil purple patches, while across her breasts and belly was a rash of crimson spots. Her face was transfixed with a look of terror as with one hand she groped under her left arm, then her mouth opened to shriek. But no sound came. Instead, as silence fell over the fans, Mandy's darkened tongue began to protrude and her knees buckled under her.

In his box Phil Jason was aghast to hear himself saying, 'She's dead! She's dead!'

7

This is Radio City and I'm Phil Jason starting my Christmas morning stint with Newsflash. *For millions of teenagers around the world it is a far from happy Yuletide following the death last night of The Strippers' lead singer. Mandy Devine, as I reported live last night, collapsed and died on stage at Wembley and so far the cause of death has not been announced. Her manager and the rest of the group are emphatic that it was not caused by a massive drug overdose. Later I'll be spinning Mandy's best-loved numbers in a special tribute.*

Reports are coming in that ambulance crews and hospital nursing staff have been asked to forgo today's holiday following an upsurge of Super flu . . .

Meanwhile, the only bright bit of news I have to offer is that an international medical team investigating the alleged germ warfare outbreak at Volkstadt have officially exonerated the East Germans – a relief to Government ministers seeking to forge closer links with East Germany. Perhaps it is this news which has inspired the Prime Minister to hold a special Cabinet meeting at Number Ten later today. This unusual move is seen by the Opposition Leader as suggesting . . .

Charity's eyes opened slowly as the familiar white figure came through the door of her small room.

'Is it Christmas Day?' she asked sleepily.

The goggled head nodded.

'So you've come to wish me Merry Christmas and let me go,' she said in the same sleepy voice while her mind struggled to become fully conscious. For the first time during the stranger's visits he had forgotten to pull the door so its automatic lock clicked from the outside.

'I see you have brought me a Santa sack,' she went on almost dreamily while under the coverlet of the hospital cot her muscles tensed for the desperate bid to get past her gaoler.

A chuckle came from behind the headpiece, but it stopped abruptly as Charity launched herself at him in a tangle of paper bedclothes. Before he realised what had happened she had rammed her knee deftly into his groin and was past him and pushing against the heavy door.

'Charity,' gasped the doubled-up figure. You've ruined me . . . For God's sake, don't open that door!'

'Paul,' she cried, swinging round. 'Paul darling!'

He rolled on to the bed.

'Oh dear, what have I done?' she exclaimed as his breath hissed painfully beneath his mask.

'Only time will tell,' he muttered. 'Open Santa's sack and get out that Ku Klux Klan rig while I try and come back to life.'

She tore at the white plastic disposal bag to find similar overalls to those he was wearing, and a cylindrical hood.

'How did you manage . . . ?' she began.

'Tell you later,' he answered. 'We've probably only got a few minutes. And much as I love you in that hospital gown, you'd better put your clothes on fast.'

Charity snatched her clothes from the narrow locker and within a minute she was fully dressed and struggling into the anti-infection suit.

'Okay,' said Paul, still taking deep breaths. 'If there's any talking to do, I'll do it.'

He eased the door open and, when Charity had slipped out behind him, locked it. Through her misting eyepieces she saw that they were in a long white corridor. At regular intervals there were similar doors, clipboards of medical notes hanging beside several of them.

'Come on.' Paul led the way down the corridor which opened into a long room. At the far end was a silvered Christmas tree, while from the central light hung a sprig of plastic mistletoe. In the corner a television set was showing an old war film, but luckily no one was watching it.

'They must be having their Christmas lunch,' Paul muttered. Charity saw that the hands of an electric clock pointed to noon, confirming her suspicion that she had been given some sedative in her food.

'Down here.'

She followed him down another passage, and her step almost faltered when she saw a man in a dark blue uniform approaching them.

'Merry Christmas,' Paul called cheerfully from behind his mask.

'And to you, doctor,' said the official. 'At least it's a white one this year.'

They walked on down the corridor, Paul pausing to look at the numbers painted on its locked doors.

'Here,' he said, glancing behind him to make sure that the man in blue had disappeared from sight. From his overalls he took a bunch of keys, checked the Dymo-taped numbers attached to them and selected one to open the door. Charity found herself following him into a pharmaceutical storeroom filled with racks of cartons and several refrigerators. At the far end was a window, partly opaqued by snow.

'Try and force it open,' Paul said. 'There's something I need in here.'

He prowled along the shelving, checking the code markings on the assorted containers. After a couple of minutes he gave an exclamation of satisfaction.

'Okay, we can make a break for it now, darling,' he said, and Charity felt a glow of pleasure that he had unconsciously used the endearment. 'Get out of your space suit.'

As he removed his own head-covering she saw that his face was thinner than she remembered it, perhaps its hollowness emphasised by its heavy growth of fair stubble.

'Wasn't trusted with a razor blade,' he explained with a ghost of his old humour. 'I'll go first. Brrr, it's freezing out here.'

Doubling up his tall frame, he squeezed through the small aperture and vanished from sight. For a moment Charity had the crazy fear that they might have been on a floor several storeys high, but a moment later the top of his head appeared level with the sill.

'I'll catch you,' he said. 'Someone up there must like us to send this snow.'

Charity jumped from the ledge into his arms and found herself in a magic world of swirling whiteness.

'I think we're in some sort of quadrangle.' His voice sounded unnaturally loud against the snow-deadened silence. 'Hold my hand, all we can do is go forward.'

Paul set off until a vague shape loomed up in front of them which turned out to be the first of a row of ambulances. He tried to open the driver's door, but it was either locked or the lock had frozen solid.

A sudden gust of wind momentarily parted the snow curtain to reveal a high wall in the middle of which was a wide entrance guarded by a small wooden office and a red and white striped barrier pole.

'Beyond that frontier post lies freedom,' he said in his half-joking voice. 'When the snow comes down again let's make a bolt for it.'

Seconds later the snow had thickened again, and all that remained to indicate the position of the gateway was a faint yellow square where electric light illuminated the office window. By now Charity was shuddering with cold and her teeth chattered as she went with Paul towards the light. Coming closer, they saw the silhouette of a human figure at the window, the slumped head suggesting that the guardian was dozing.

'Here we go,' Paul whispered, leading Charity round the barrier pole.

'Hey,' came a voice from the office. 'You two . . . '

'Yes?' Paul answered pleasantly.

'Ain't they finished the first lunch sitting yet? I'm starving to death out here.'

'They're just on the Christmas pud,' Charity said with what she hoped sounded like an innocent laugh. 'I'm sure you'll be relieved in a minute. The turkey was delicious. Merry Christmas.'

'It may be for some,' said the man darkly and slammed his window shut. As the fugitives walked through the gateway they heard the muffled trilling of a telephone.

Paul glanced briefly back at the gateway and saw on the arch above it the sculpted words 'St John's Fever Hospital'.

'Look at that,' he exclaimed. 'And I had no idea where we were. We must have been in the special wing.'

Holding on to each other to stop themselves slipping in the snow, they ran along the deserted footpath beside the humps of snow-covered parked cars.

'From what I remember when we made our raid here, there should be an Underground station down this road,' Charity said.

'A few minutes later they reached it, but an iron grille blocked its entrance.

'Of course, the tube doesn't run on Christmas Day,' she exclaimed. 'We'll just have to keep walking.'

The freezing flakes thinned, then stopped, and they found themselves walking through a world which the snow had made surreal.

'We could be the last people left alive in London,' said Charity. 'Now, tell me . . . '

'Nothing much to tell. This morning our sinister visitor in white made the mistake of turning his back on me and I jumped him. I guess he thought I was too tranquillised to be a danger, but in fact I'd been flushing my food down the lavatory. So I tied him up with the sheets, put on his outfit and locked him in my room. I worked my way down the corridor, opening the doors of the isolation rooms until I found you. On the way I picked up an extra set of overalls from a store cupboard.'

'You make it sound so simple.'

'It was. But I don't know how long it will be before our gaoler is missed. Let's hope he was scheduled for the second sitting of the festive lunch . . . '

'But what could they do now that we are out? We've been cooped up for three days and it's obvious I've got no infectious disease . . . '

'There are charges against me for interfering with a corpse,' said Paul with a dry laugh. 'Though if plague has really broken out they may not be interested in us any more. I've no idea what has been happening in the outside world. The thing-from-outer-space refused to answer my questions . . . Hey, look there.'

Down the silent road came a beautiful red double-decker bus.

Charity glanced round in vain for a bus stop, then ran into the middle of the road with her arms wide.

The bus ground to a halt on the gritted surface.

'Thanks, brother,' she shouted to the black driver.

'Okay, sister,' he shouted back. 'I'm what they call the skeleton service, so get your bones aboard.'

'Where does this bus go to?' Paul asked the conductor as they started up.

'Shepherd's Bush, mate.'

'Great,' said Charity. 'We'll keep you company to Notting Hill . . . '

Upstairs she said to Paul, 'My flat's in Ladbroke Square.'

For a moment the snow on each side of the road reflected blue light. Anxiously Paul looked out of the rear window but it was no police car, only a pair of ambulances racing to overtake the bus.

'Seen a lot of them this morning.' said the conductor. 'Must have been some disaster. Ever noticed there's always a disaster at Christmas?'

Charity led Paul up three flights of narrow stairs, unlocked a door on a small landing and ushered him into her flat. It was just what he had subconsciously expected – a mixture of the very practical and the exotic. The walls of the living room were decorated with oriental rugs and the polished floor was scattered with animal skins bought from time to time at sales. Disconcertingly, one wall was a mirror and she explained, before he could read any erotic interpretation into it that the previous owner had been a ballet dancer. Opposite the mirror was a profusion of tropical plants, which she affectionately referred to as her mini-jungle. On entering the room she greeted them as other people would household pets.

'I'm going to run a bath for you,' she told Paul. 'You're blue with cold, and while you're soaking I'll fix us some hot soup. Then we can decide what we're going to do.'

He found the bathroom to be the most interesting room in the flat. There were spotlights, gold-tinted mirrors, a sunken bath and more plants thrusting long tendrils from an antique *jardinière*.

Along a back-lit shelf was a row of cut-glass bottles containing bath essences and unguents and several glass wall cabinets held a vast array of cosmetics. On one shelf stood a figurine of Mercury which he recognised as a Broadcast Award – probably for the campaign she had conducted against genetic engineering, he decided ruefully.

Charity turned on the taps and soon perfumed steam was rising from the bath.

'I'll bring you a drink – I think we both deserve one,' she said and disappeared in the direction of the kitchenette which Paul found later to be a wonderland of gadgetry.

'You like Sibelius, I seem to remember,' she called, and suddenly from concealed speakers the opening bars of the *Tapiola* filled the bathroom.

Gratefully Paul sank into steaming water, its heat soothing away the cold that had made his limbs tremble. A minute later Charity appeared with glasses which matched her essence bottles.

'Nothing like brandy and soda to guard against snake bite,' she said.

'Join me,' he said. 'You look perished.'

Unselfconsciously she removed her sodden clothing, and Paul felt the same sense of delight as he had on *Blue Flame* at the sight of her lithe, darkly bronze body.

'That's better,' she smiled as she lowered herself beneath the outrageously expensive bubble foam.

'Here's to us,' she added as they clinked their glasses.

'Do many people know your address?' he asked.

She shook her head.

'Apart from some friends only The Digger. Why?'

'I was wondering whether we are likely to be traced here,' Paul said. 'They seemed damned keen on keeping us incommunicado . . . '

'I'm sure it was Vic Kelly who warned the authorities I would use the *Guest Host* programme to break the story, so

I suppose he might give my address to the Special Branch or whoever . . . '

'They could trace you through your telephone,' said Paul. 'I think once we've thawed out we should visit a friend of mine in the country.'

'Let's thaw first,' said Charity with a smile that Paul thought was delightfully wicked.

Dressed again, and with a feeling of well-being which was not entirely due to the drink in his hand, Paul gazed out over Ladbroke Square. On the opposite side, her shoulders bowed by the weight of a bulging bag, an old woman shuffled like a refugee on a journey to nowhere. The railed garden in the centre was without a hint of colour and the delicate tracery of its leafless trees suggested the frosted forest of a pantomime. In her kitchenette Charity was cooking to the sound of carols from her radio.

'Anything I can do?' he called.

'Just relax. I'm trying to doctor up this packet soup with herbs.'

Gratefully Paul stretched himself out on a sofa and continued to gaze over the tops of the magical trees to the darkening sky. It must have been the confinement, he told himself, which caused his back to ache. He had missed his usual routine of pre-breakfast jogging.

'Paul,' called Charity. 'While we were isolated I was told that the slide you had at the television studio was a fake.'

'That's right, it was blank,' he answered cheerfully. 'I brought it along for dramatic effect.'

'But, you can't mean . . . '

'You don't think I was going to risk carrying a slide of plague bacilli, do you?' he laughed. 'The real slide is safely stored at the Coram lab. It held enough bugs to start an epidemic if they got loose. In fact, I've been thinking deeply about that slide and . . . '

'Don't let's talk about such beastly things just as we are about to eat,' said Charity, bringing in a tray on which two blue patterned bowls of soup steamed.

Paul got up awkwardly.

'I must have strained my back climbing out of that window or something,' he muttered. 'I'll take some aspirin later. I say, this looks rather splendid.'

'I'm afraid there's only canned things to follow. Still, it's our first Christmas dinner together.'

'Then here's to it and the next one,' he said, raising his glass.

Suddenly a sombre voice interrupted the choir.

'This is Radio City with a special announcement.'

'That's Trevor Jones,' said Charity. 'I've always thought it's his ambition to announce World War III.'

'Sounds like he's going to do it now.'

'Following a special Cabinet meeting in two hours' time, the Prime Minister is to make an important broadcast at seven o'clock this evening,' Trevor Jones was saying. 'The scheduled tribute to Mandy Devine will now be broadcast at a slightly later date. And now back to the choir of King's College . . . '

'What can have happened to Mandy?' cried Charity. 'I've lost touch with the outside world.' As if to contradict her the telephone began to ring.

They jumped nervously, its insistent call coming like a threat into the brief spell of warmth and happiness they had woven together.

'That's the outside world,' said Paul grimly.

They sat still while it continued to ring, Charity fighting a mad inclination to pick it up if only to break the tension it was causing.

After a minute it stopped.

'I think we should leave,' said Paul regretfully. 'I want to take that plague slide down to my old guru Sir Robert McAusland in Dorset. He's semi-retired, lives alone, and I'm sure he'd be pleased to put us up at his place near Charlton Marshall.'

'If you say so,' said Charity with a sigh.

There had been no problem in retrieving the bacilli slide which was now stored in a specially insulated container in the boot of Charity's Mercedes. Paul had half expected to be surrounded by policemen as he let himself into the Bloomsbury laboratory, but the only hint of life had been the distant hee-haw of a receding ambulance.

Now, as Charity drove past Madame Tussauds on Marylebone Road, a blue flicker in her mirror caused her to pull over and another ambulance hurtled past, spraying the white convertible with slush.

'I've never seen so many ambulances.'

'You may be seeing a lot more,' said Paul who yet again was hunting through the wavebands of her radio. Radio City was restricting itself to light music interspersed with advertisments, and the BBC stations were equally non-committal in presenting their typical Christmas programmes.

'Something bad's happening,' said Charity as she accelerated down deserted Park Lane. 'My Voices tell me.'

'And I've a pretty good idea what it is,' added Paul as they swept round Hyde Park Corner and he saw another winking blue light vanishing down Piccadilly.

For a while they drove without speaking while he continued to turn the tuning knob.

'Oh leave it,' said Charity with sudden irritation. 'We'll know soon enough. If I were not *persona non grata* I'd ring up the station – they must have a clue as to what's happening.'

'It's hard to picture before the event how a calamity actually starts,' Paul mused as they passed Harrods which was outlined by thousands of yellow lights, so that for a second they were *Arabian Nights* travellers before the gloom of Brompton Road closed upon them. 'The Great Plague began gradually, and people followed its progress through the weekly Bills of Mortality. A couple of cases, then nothing for six weeks, then another and then each week an increasing number of burials in the parishes of St Giles-in-the-Fields and in Holborn. It was not until several months had gone by that the epidemic began to really grip the city and the exodus began. This time it'll be like an explosion . . . '

'Paul, please be quiet. We haven't all got your scientific detachment.' He turned to look at her curiously and saw in the glow of the instruments that her eyes were dangerously moist.

'Oh, I'm sorry,' he said awkwardly. 'I didn't mean to scare you . . . '

'I wasn't thinking about myself,' she retorted. 'Some of us have families and people we care about . . . '

Then it was her turn to be contrite as she remembered that Paul, an only child, had been orphaned at an early age and had been forced to be a loner whether he liked it or not. She felt very sorry for him not having enjoyed the boisterous and secure family life she had known. For a while they drove in silence.

'I was exaggerating . . . '

'Where are all the cars coming from?'

They spoke simultaneously to break the uncomfortable silence as they skirted the Old Deer Park and headed south-west towards the M3. Now, instead of having the road to themselves, they became part of a very fast moving stream of traffic. From every side-road tributary, cars – usually of the expensive type – queued with revving engines to join the mainstream.

Suddenly the traffic line jerked to a halt and several vehicles shunted into each other as their tyres failed to grip on the slush. Ahead, Charity saw that the driver of a Jaguar, losing patience, had pulled out in the path of a racing Morgan. Unable to stop, the nose of the sports car rammed the side of the larger one. Locked by a tangle of twisted metal, the vehicles slid in a circular motion and came to rest with the Jaguar up on the pavement.

Traffic began to flow round the distorted machines while from the smashed windscreen of the Jaguar a bloodied arm flapped as though waving farewell. The Alpine horns of the Morgan blared on and on like the death wail of a dinosaur.

'They're getting rough,' said Charity, her knuckles tightening on the leather-bound wheel as a car surged past on the inside, then crazily swerved in front of her in order to miss a parked van.

'Bastard!' muttered Paul, feeling the Mercedes slide slightly as Charity expertly slowed it without going into a full skid.

'We'll be on the M3 soon, darling,' she said calmly. 'Then they won't be able to come at us from the sides.'

Ahead traffic lights glowed red and the Mercedes rolled to a halt, its front wheels level with a traffic island, and at that moment Paul and Charity were jerked in their seat belts as they were slammed from behind. In the mirror Paul saw the door of the offending car burst open and a beefy-faced man ran to Charity's window and pummelled it with his fist.

'Bloody cow,' he shouted. 'What the sodding hell did you have to stop for?'

Calmly she pointed at the red light.

'Why the hell stop for that, you black bitch?' he raved, continuing to pound the glass.

Paul felt something inside him grow terribly cold. Carefully he removed his glasses and placed them in the glove-box, then in a second he was outside and round the car, tapping the big man on the shoulder. Intent on abusing Charity, he turned with a surprised expression on his face.

Unhurriedly Paul put out his left arm and waved his fingers in front of the man's eyes, so that by reflex action he threw up his hands to protect his face. While thus unguarded, Paul slammed a short-arm jab into his gut which made the breath whistle out of his throat. He fell flat on his back in the dirty snow.

Paul returned to his seat, and as the light turned to green the Mercedes shot forward, leaving the man floundering in front of his aghast family.

'Thank you, my knight errant.'

Paul shrugged and replaced his glasses.

'Do you know the really dreadful thing about that?' he said. 'He was in his bedroom slippers!'

8

Men and women of Britain, in addressing you from Number 10 Downing Street tonight I am bringing you the most heart-rending message possible for a Prime Minister apart from an announcement of war.

I regret to inform you that in London during the last twenty-four hours over five hundred people have died of the bubonic plague, and several thousand have been hospitalised, some of whom are very seriously ill. At this point it is imperative to reassure you that this outbreak is in no way connected with the spurious rumour of a germ warfare disaster in the Democratic Republic of Germany. There can be no doubt that some local source is responsible for the London epidemic . . .

Paul's mind wandered as he listened to the avuncular voice of the Prime Minister while Charity's Mercedes sped down the M3 with the speedo needle quivering nervously around the 90 mph. mark. In the outside lane an endless stream of cars was overtaking her, horns wailing in anguish as drivers sought to go even faster.

And in each metal box hurtling through the snowy night that voice is announcing doom, Paul thought. Each has its own hotline from Nemesis. Strange how the panic spread before the official announcement to trigger this high-speed exodus. The same motorway madness must be taking place on all roads leading out of London.

'. . . naturally it goes without saying that the Government and the GLC are doing everything possible to combat the outbreak,' the Premier continued. 'Contingency plans were formulated when the first case was suspected several days ago, and these are being put into operation. Special medical teams have been organised and plague serum is being flown in from countries where plague is endemic, for which I express heartfelt gratitude on behalf of us all . . . '

Paul snorted.

'There isn't enough serum in the world to inoculate a quarter of London,' he said.

' . . . and the fact that details of the isolated cases which preceded this outbreak were not presented to the media was the result of much careful consideration. The apprehension of myself, my Cabinet colleagues and the GLC Health Department was that a pre-emptive announcement would serve no useful purpose and the resultant panic only increase danger to life and property.'

'Hypocrite!' Charity cried. 'They just hoped it would go away. Oh Paul, I'm getting scared, everyone's driving like maniacs.'

' . . . frequent radio and television broadcasts will provide you with up-to-date information and practical advice. Ministry of Health experts stress that members of the public resident within the confines of London should remain in their own homes and avoid mingling in crowds in which contagion might be transmitted by the breath. To encourage this, it has been agreed with London Transport and the appropriate unions that the Christmas Day close-down of services will be maintained for at least several days, and I am grateful that, if this visitation had to descend upon us, it came at this moment in time when the least number of people have to attend their places of work because of seasonal holidays.

'The necessity of preventing the infection spreading to the rest of Britain cannot be over-stressed and to this end I beg you all most sincerely to refrain from leaving the capital in the mistaken belief that by doing so you will be at less risk. If you have unfortunately already contracted the disease leaving London will not help you. Everybody will be safest by quietly remaining at home and co-operating with your local authorities' immunisation schemes. Following this broadcast you will be given details of these, the procedures to carry out in case of emergency and notification of the special powers it has been considered necessary to grant to the Metropolitan and Greater London police forces.

'Finally, I believe that your elected Government, with the backing of Trade Unions, our magnificent health service and the working people of this country, will overcome this biological threat with the same spirit and determination that triumphed in the dark days of Dunkirk. Let us draw comfort from the curious fact that the British character is at its best under adversity.'

'So now it's out officially,' said Charity. 'It makes my attempt to break the story seem pointless.'

'You certainly had a good try,' Paul said. 'And if it had worked you might have saved thousands of lives . . . '

'Do you mean that seriously? Thousands?'

'Oh yes. If the public had been aware of the danger at the start of the incubation period, instead of being fobbed off with lies about Super flu, proper preparations could have been made – immunisation schemes in high risk areas and immediate treatment of the slightest suspect symptoms. I think most people ignored the Super flu warnings. Flu is something that comes regularly at Christmas and which you get over with Lemsip and a few days in bed. But they wouldn't have ignored honest warnings about plague.'

'So what do we do now?'

'Turn off at the next junction, this is getting too scary.'

Even as he spoke a car in front of the Mercedes tried to accelerate into a gap in the fast lane, with the result that a Volvo struck its rear wing and sent it sliding back into the central lane. Through whirlpools of snowflakes created by the traffic slipstream, Paul and Charity saw fists waving through glass and mouths agape with mindless abuse.

On the central reservation a warning light blinked a message to stop, but the rushing traffic was blind to it. On the hard shoulder a white police car was parked with lights flashing while a policeman shouted incomprehensibly through a loudhailer.

'I want out of this race,' said Charity, and Paul knew her well enough by now to recognise that the very lightness of her tone covered her fear – fear of being trapped in this speeding stream of steel.

'I wonder how the word spread to so many before the official admission came out,' he said, trying to take her mind off the cacophony of horns battering their eardrums as cars fought to overtake each other.

'I guess it was the Citizens' Band grapevine,' said Charity. 'Obviously people involved must have talked – ambulance men and hospital workers – and once the rush started the word would get broadcast. Turn on the CB and see what they're saying – the tuner is under the glovebox.'

Paul switched on and immediately a babel of hysterical voices filled the car. It reminded him of a 'disaster' movie he had once seen about a sinking ship, with a sound-track enriched by the shouts and yells of people trapped below decks.

As he sifted through the forty CB wavebands broken phrases came through before being submerged in the general hubbub.

'The smoky bears are up ahead, but I'm keeping my foot heavy . . . '

'Champagne Cork here – no dice on the M1, it's clogged . . . '

'Will some friend tell me what the hell . . . '

'Sandra, I'm trying to make it home . . . don't open the door to no one . . . Sandra, hear me . . . don't open . . . '

Paul turned to Band 9, the band which by the code of the CB users was always left for emergency calls only. Immediately a frightened voice whispered from the speaker, though even in his moment of distress the caller continued to use his code name.

'Pussycat calling Mayday . . . Pussycat calling Mayday . . . I'm on the hard shoulder west of the Windsor turnoff, and I'm coughing blood . . . Could some friend send help, I think I'm dying . . . Pussycat calling Mayday . . . Pussycat . . . '

His voice was drowned out by a burst of static and then another voice shouting in panic. A second later these words ended in a crash as though a cupboard full of crockery had spilled on to a stone floor.

Paul turned off and glanced at Charity. Perspiration

dewed her forehead.

'I feel like a reluctant lemming,' she said with an attempt at a grin. 'What now?'

The traffic about them was slowing, as though at last heeding the stop symbol of the motorway hazard lights.

Soon it was obvious that the way ahead was blocked. When it came to the Mercedes' turn to halt, Paul climbed out and saw a great tangle of cars about five hundred yards ahead. The vehicles had not merely shunted into an instant junkyard, they had reared up like frenzied animals trying to climb on each others' backs in panic.

'My God . . . Oh, my God,' repeated the driver of the car which had pulled up beside the Mercedes. The thunder of racing traffic faded. From behind came an occasional crash as cars braked too late or too hard and slid into those already parked, from ahead the cold wind brought a faint chorus of voices distorted by agony and fear.

'It's like a bloody breaker's yard,' the driver exclaimed. Paul turned to him and saw the frightened faces of two young children peering out through the windscreen while in the back a young woman sat nursing a baby.'

'Got the tip off from my brother-in-law,' said the man, anxious to talk, to explain, to make contact with another refugee. 'He's in the undertaking line . . . '

'Hey, mate, give us a hand. We can't stay stuck here.'

Paul turned and saw they were almost opposite a gap in the central crash barrier. It was blocked by a line of metal posts which could be removed by the police or firemen should they need to turn on to the opposite carriageway in an emergency. A burly driver was straining to get the first one out of its socket. From several of the stranded cars drivers ran to help him.

'Any moment now that bloody scrap heap is going to go up,' he shouted as Paul bent beside him to lend a hand. 'You can smell the petrol from here.'

The opposite carriageway was comparatively empty, and cars coming up it slowed as their drivers gazed incredulously at the acres of wreckage blocking the westbound lanes. In the distance there was an erratic sprinkling of blue lights as fire engines and ambulances rushed towards the scene.

'What the hell do you think you're doing?'

Paul and the other men looked up to see a motorcycle policeman running down the central reservation. The beam of his powerful torch flitted over them as they strove to remove the barrier which prevented them from making a break on to the empty carriageway.

'What does it look like we're doing?' growled the man who had started the work. 'We're getting out, mate.'

'I must warn you that you're committing an offence,' said the policeman, whose youth and tension made him take refuge in officialese. 'Under the motorways regulations . . . '

'Piss off!'

'I warn you that . . . that you are obstructing a police officer in the execution of his duty,' the policeman told the burly driver who was still struggling to unseat the last barrier post.

The man straightened triumphantly, the metal post in his arms. The policeman stepped forward, one arm outstretched, but before he could say another word the man hurled the post straight at him. It caught him across the chest and sent him reeling through the gap. There was a wail of air horns, a scream of brakes which to Paul seemed to go on for ever and ever, then a sickening thump as the policeman went under a truck.

For a moment a white face looked down from the cab, then the truck roared off into the darkness, leaving a dark bundle huddled between broad tracks etched on the sprinkling of snow. Alone of the men Paul started towards the sprawled figure, until he saw that a heavy-duty tyre had flattened its head to a dark smear. Choking on the bile which scorched his throat, he stumbled back to the Mercedes.

Already the man who had flung the bar was manoeuvring his car through the gap. Around them engines revved and drivers inched forward, jealous of their places in the queue to escape the jammed carriageway. A frenzy of hooting recalled Charity to reality and the fact that it was her turn to swing through the opening.

'Best to go back to London,' said Paul. 'This is . . . '

His words were blown away by the shockwave of an explosion. From the centre of the tangled cars orange flames fountained into the black sky as, somewhere among the twisted machines, a spark from a broken electrical circuit ignited the petrol slick from burst tanks.

Following the initial blast, a curtain of fire danced across both carriageways, swamping the lights of approaching rescue teams. People sprang from cars parked ahead of the Mercedes and fled between stationary vehicles in terror. Some raced along the empty east-bound carriageway, others leapt down the embankment to fields spreading towards the distant glitter of a town.

'Go, Charity, go,' cried Paul as the conflagration swept towards them, fed by the exploding tanks of the cars it consumed. Through its roar came shrieks from those trapped in their distorted vehicles or too paralysed by terror to get out and run.

Behind the wheel Charity sat immobile, gazing at the approaching fire tsunami with wide eyes.

'Through the gap!' Paul shouted, as he felt an invisible wall of heat strike them, but his words did not seem to register with her. It was as though the awful vision had her spellbound.

It was the shock of the car behind ramming their boot that jerked her out of her trance. She switched the engine into life and, wrenching the wheel to its full lock, put her foot down and accelerated through the breach. Paul winced with horror as he felt the wheels lurch over the policeman's corpse, but mercifully Charity did not know what it was. The convertible, its white paint no longer immaculate, its body battered, sped at a hundred miles an hour towards the sky-glow marking London. Behind them flames leapt jubilantly as, fanned by the black wind, they engulfed row after row of cars like the flames of hell sucking the damned to their doom.

The Mercedes rolled to a halt on the south side of Ladbroke Square. With a sigh of relief Paul switched off the ignition and saw that Charity was still asleep in the fleece-covered passenger seat, having been too exhausted to drive after escaping the holocaust. With the windscreen wipers at rest, fine snow began to coat the glass and Paul pressed his fingertips over his taut face, relishing the silence which came with the snowflakes. The mental picture which had tortured him for the last hour – the headless body of the policeman, the screams of the family in the car parked beside them – dissolved in stillness, and peace filled him as he looked at Charity's relaxed face beside him.

He fought the inclination to close his eyes and doze off beside her. He had the strange sensation that at any moment he would float away as though filled with some lighter-than-air gas. For a moment everything appeared to be in slow motion. He watched his hand rise centimetre by centimetre from the wheel until it finally touched Charity's cheek.

He shook his head. What was happening? Obviously the stress of the day had drained him, but he must get Charity to her flat before he fell asleep otherwise they might be found frozen in the car. But again his thoughts wavered, and the idea of such a death seemed strangely fascinating. He had read how explorers in arctic lands were tempted to lie down and sleep in snowstorms. There was an allure in the cold purity of death's gentlest touch.

For a moment Paul felt he was no longer in the car but alone in a northern forest, a forest conjured by the music of Sibelius, and to whose corporate life he was gladly surrendering his own. . . .

He sneezed violently, and the spasm shook him back to reality.

'I'm dreaming before I'm properly asleep, he thought.

'Come along, darling,' he said aloud. 'We're home now.'

'That was a terrific sneeze you woke me with,' she said. 'I hope you're not getting the flu . . .' She stopped. 'Let's get some proper sleep,' she added lamely.

She led the way up the three flights of stairs and they entered her flat.

Paul looked about him with approval.

'Don't let's talk about anything,' he said. 'Sufficient unto the day is the evil thereof . . . Oh,' he added, stretching, 'my back is killing me.'

She took him by the hand and led him into the bedroom, pulling back the great fur rug which covered her bed.

'I don't know what it is, Charity,' Paul said, 'but something smells very nice up here.'

'What?' she exclaimed.

'The air smells sweet,' he said and smiled at her.

'Oh, my darling!' she exclaimed. 'Get into bed at once.'

'Charity, for goodness' sake, why are you looking at me like that? You're not crying, are you?'

Pale light filtered through the Venetian blinds as Paul gratefully opened his eyes. The sleep he had desired so much had been riddled with dreams, dreams which had translated the semi-wakeful hallucinations he had experienced into nightmares. Again he had been in a forest, but this time the branches of Upas trees held him while tendrils flowed down his throat and into his lungs to suck his life. Again he had lived through the events of the M3, but this time the policeman was already headless when he came running towards them, torch in hand. Again he had felt the wall of heat strike the Mercedes as the river of flame flowed towards them.

Thank God dreams were over, yet the sense of heat remained.

'Charity,' he murmured, aware that his voice sounded odd. 'Darling . . . have you . . . got a ther . . . thermometer . . . ?'

To his surprise she was not in the big bed, but, dressed in a floppy white sweater and tight velvet jeans, was sitting beside him, her face a study of anxiety.

'I'll get it,' she said and disappeared in the direction of the bathroom. A couple of minutes later she took a clinical thermometer from his mouth and held it up to the light.

'A hundred and five!' she gasped. 'Darling . . . '

'I've got it,' Paul said. He tried to give her a grin. 'I should say it's got me. That spill in the lab.'

'Paul, I'll get an ambulance right away.'

He tried to rise up on one elbow, to call her back, but his body began to tremble violently and he dropped down.

Minutes dragged by. From afar he heard Charity say a few words between great intervals of silence, but the hallucinations were returning and when she came back into the room he had the momentary illusion that she had grown wings and was rising on them to the ceiling. A moment later his eyes refocussed and the scene in the room was back to normal.

'I dialled 999,' she said. 'They gave me a special emergency number, but the line is endlessly engaged. I'll keep trying, but what can I do until I get through?'

With a great effort Paul spoke calmly, enunciating his words with care to try and avoid the slurring caused by a swollen tongue. He asked her to open his case and take out a hypodermic syringe and the packet he had stolen from St John's pharmacy.

'Please unpack it,' he said. 'It's streptomycin. Only wish I'd thought to nick morphia while I was at it. Pass it to me, then I want you to leave the room and keep clear of me. I can inject myself . . . '

She told him not to be ridiculous and propped him up against pillows so he could load the syringe, but when she saw how his hands trembled she took it from him and asked the dosage. Carefully she drew back the plunger and asked him what to do next.

'Squirt a drop out to get rid of the bubble,' he muttered. 'Then intramuscular . . . push the needle into my arm . . . and . . . and . . . just press . . . '

'I'll try not to hurt,' said Charity, though at the thought of giving an injection she felt sick.

'Just pump it in.'

She placed the needle against the skin of his upper arm. When she pressed, the point did not slide into the flesh but merely made a depression in the skin.

'You . . . have to push . . . quite hard.'

Closing her eyes, Charity did as she was told. She felt resistance for a moment, then the skin was pierced and the needle was vanishing into her lover's arm. A thought came which made her damp with sweat – supposing she struck an artery! Would a jet of blood result?

Looking away, she held the syringe with the fingers of

her left hand and steadily depressed the plunger with her right.

As she withdrew the needle Paul lost consciousness and she was painfully aware of the rasping in his throat. She hurried back to the telephone, dialled the special number and stood while minute after minute the engaged signal buzzed in her ear.

9

The time is exactly three o'clock and this is Radio City with an emergency bulletin, read by Phil Jason: As a result of a panic exodus from London last night more lives were lost in traffic accidents and motorway pile-ups than have been claimed by the plague. All motorways leading out of the capital are blocked with wreckage, and on the M3 alone several hundred cars were burnt out. The police announce that motorways will remain closed until further notice.

In his dove-grey office Vic Kelly turned down the relay loudspeaker and looked moodily over his desk at the two key men in his station. They were in complete contrast to each other – Tim Holt, the programme controller, was young, keen-faced and immaculately suited; Raymond Carson was twenty years older and looked more. With a face that friends described kindly as 'lived in', he didn't give a damn about his appearance. Vic noticed that in buttoning up his ghastly cardigan he had not got the buttons in the right holes. But behind his coarsened features was a highly intelligent and experienced news editor whom Vic had bribed away from Fleet Street at tremendous expense.

'There'll be one of these bulletins on the hour every hour,' Tim Holt said. 'I can tell you it's meant some tricky rescheduling, but I reckon the ad boys can sell the spots each side of them as prime time. I'm thinking of a daily half-hour programme called *Lifeline* in which people who've lost touch with families or friends in the panic can phone in with messages. This should get us a peak audience. Tonight after the Archbishop of Canterbury's broadcast, I want to repeat Charity's Plague Village piece. What a lucky coincidence that was – makes you believe!'

Vic nodded.

'I just wish to hell I knew where that Sheila is,' he said. 'All I know is she took to the hills with Frankenstein. I want her found, Ray. Can you put a bloke on to it?'

The news editor looked doubtful.

'I'm short-staffed already,' he said. 'The flu took its toll this Christmas – and some of those off sick may have something worse. Those still on their feet are hard at it because we can't rely on official releases. I reckon they're holding back the real death totals. I had a tip off, for example, that half the ambulance crews are down with plague, and it's decimated the staff of hospitals where cases were admitted early on. We're in for a grim time and I wonder how many of us will see the end of it.'

Without a word Vic went to his drinks cabinet and poured out the favourite drinks of his two lieutenants.

'From now on it's going to be a bastard, but let's have one together for old times's sake,' he said. 'We've built up a pretty fair station and if we fell out over some things at least we had a few laughs as well. Here's to us!'

They raised their glasses.

'You've told the staff that anyone who wants to quit won't be held to contract?'

'A couple of the married typists with kids want to stay at home – understandable,' Tim said. 'Everyone else seems to have the Alamo spirit.'

'In a funny sort of way they're excited,' said the news editor. 'This is the story of the century.'

'That's for sure,' said The Digger. 'Now, Ray, what I want compiled is a daily feature we can syndicate round the world like those old broadcasts about the London Blitz I heard in Wagga Wagga as a kid. The old Brit grit in coping with man's most terrible enemy! Vivid word pictures!

They'll probably have to have dead carts soon, and maybe plague pits!'

'Talking about that, I had a leak from the Health Department on how the plague may have started,' said Raymond. 'I think we can turn on the heat with this one and roll heads. I'm working on the possibility that the germs had hibernated since the Great Plague.'

'I sure need Charity for the syndication,' said Vic. 'She's got just the right human interest approach. Facts and figures will soon be meaningless. What we want is stories people abroad can relate to . . . families stricken, kids orphaned, heroes and heroines – the Eyam story all over again.'

Ray's pocket phone buzzed and he held it to his ear for a moment, then he made a characteristic gesture of striking his palm with a balled fist.

'It's hotting up, Digger,' he said. 'The PM is recalling MPs from the Christmas recess . . . to Edinburgh.'

Outside, a still snowy Ludgate Circus shared the uncanny silence which hung over London. The spasm of terror which had sent so many drivers hurtling out of the capital had passed, and now Londoners were spending Boxing Day in a curious exhausted calm. In most homes families watched the BBC's presentation of *The Sound of Music*, fairy lights glittered on millions of Christmas trees and, apart from the radio bulletins and the BBC and ITN news pictures of the motorway carnage, the threat of plague became momentarily unreal.

As an anti-panic measure eminent authorities explained on the special bulletins that while there was no denying several hundred people had died as a result of *Pasteurella pestis,* it was an infinitesimal proportion of London's huge population. After all, the dead numbered no more than would be expected in a Jumbo crash. Now that the disease was correctly diagnosed, modern medicine would ensure that nothing like the visitation of 1665 could recur.

So bland were these experts that many listeners and viewers were reassured enough to forget the fear that had come with the Prime Minister's announcement the day before. Had these same listeners and viewers been aware of the preparations being made behind the scenes they might not have been so calm.

Turning from Ladbroke Grove into a side street, Charity parked her car where a diminutive Asian woman in a blue sari scraped the window of the grocery store which she had run with her husband since arriving in London as victims of an Africanisation programme. Across the glass, behind which was a homely confusion of plastic toys, cat litter, soft drinks and 'special offer' tinned foods, tall letters in aerosol day-glo proclaimed IMIGRANTS = BUBONIK PLAGUE.

'Oh, Mrs Patel!' cried Charity in dismay.

'It's the NBP,' said Mrs Patel sadly. 'They blame us for the sickness. Now come inside, my dear. What do you need? Buy while you can – bad times are ahead.'

Charity left the Patel shop with a heavy heart and the boot of the Mercedes loaded with enough provisions to last her and Paul for at least a fortnight. After this one trip she did not want to leave him again until she was sure the antibiotics she injected regularly had defeated the organisms attacking his body.

Returning to the flat, she found he had awoken from a feverish sleep.

'Do you feel any better, darling?' She touched his forehead and was shocked to feel how hot and dry it was.

'Charity.' He spoke with great difficulty. 'You must not stay.'

'We've been through all that, Paul.'

'But . . . but I'm breathing out poison.'

'I've been with you long enough to have caught it from you if I was going to.'

'I don't understand it . . . Wish we could've reached McAusland . . . there's something wrong . . . '

His voice trailed away, and his eyelids drooped as he returned to an uneasy sleep.

In the next room the telephone began to ring again.

After Boxing Day the weather changed. The sky above

London took on a luminous watercolour blue and the midday sun, although not warm enough to melt the snow which remained in Hyde Park, gave a Scandinavian brilliance to the city. At Speakers' Corner the breath of the single constable rose like pale smoke as he stamped his feet and kept his eye dispassionately on the two groups who had braved the cold to proclaim their message.

He missed his old favourites, the Pyramidologist, the man who claimed the government owed him a million pounds for an invention, the shaggy-haired prophet who quoted the Book of Revelations to predict the world's end and the beautifully dressed lady whose lecture on harmonic vibrations he never understood.

Today the New Britain Party enthusiasts were in their accustomed place near the Underground exit, a phalanx of dark figures facing a speaker on a portable rostrum hung with a large Union Jack.

'It's a lie to call us racist,' said Lancelot Storm. 'The New Britain Party has nothing against Jews or black people – in their own countries. What we denounce is the dark tide which has swept into this country, and let me ask you a question – is a true-born Christian Englishman allowed to become a citizen of Jamaica, Israel or Pakistan? It's they who are the racists! It is they, comrades-in-arms, who have brought their filthy diseases into our once-fair land – a land which will be fair again when the sleeping might of its native sons is awakened . . .'

The constable turned away.

He felt like shouting, 'You're too late – your dreams died in a Berlin bunker forty years ago.' But he kept his face impassive despite the fact that his grandparents had died in Dachau.

The other group was religious. A gloomy banner proclaimed them as Evangelical Dissenters, and a cadaverous preacher regarded his flock belligerently from his step-ladder as he promised hell-fire and doom.

This was more to the constable's sense of humour, and at least the religious freaks were harmless. He stood at the back of the crowd, rubbing his gloved hands together and enjoying the incongruity of the speaker's message with his ill-fitting dental plate. When his rhetoric took flight the front row of the faithful pressed back to avoid his free-flying spittle.

'For my text today I have turned to the sixteenth chapter of Numbers – verse 46 – which tell us, " . . . for there is wrath gone out from the Lord; the plague is begun." Think on it, brothers and sisters, think on the truth of those words *the plague is begun*. This is no warning of what *may* happen if Man continues his sinning, I tell you it's too late for that . . .'

The preacher's eyes lit up with pleasure at the thought.

'THE PLAGUE IS BEGUN!' he thundered while his adherents cringed. 'And why is the plague begun? Because the message of God was ignored, because murder and perversion have been made lawful, because Man has preferred vile pornography to the Holy Writ, because so-called Christians have turned to false faiths – the Mormons, the Jehovah's Witnesses, the Seventh day Adventists – the list is long and abominable – and . . .' here his voice lowered dramatically while the flock busied themselves with their handkerchiefs '. . . and above all the false Church of Rome and its lackey the Church of England. Oh yes, brothers and sisters, we have been scorned, our message has been ignored down the years, but now we can look about us and see that as the servants of the Lord we were right – *the plague is begun*!'

A chorus of alleluias followed and an American on the edge of the throng looked anxiously at the sound level meter of his portable recorder.

The preacher became almost conversational.

'Brothers and sisters, let's see what else the good book has to tell us.'

He opened his Bible and read, ' "And I looked, and beheld a pale horse: and his name that sat on him was Death, and Hell followed him."

'I hope I don't need to tell you where that text comes from or who the rider of the pale horse is – he is the pestilence that the Good Lord sendeth to cleanse His world. And have you thought what will follow that Pale Horse and his Awful Rider?

'Friends, I can give you a hint because the Lord in His mercy showed Man what to expect if he did not turn to the light.

'Three hundred years ago that great dissenting writer Daniel Defoe recorded the full horror of the pestilence, and he tells us, brothers and sisters, what the ungodly can expect.'

Opening his Bible he took out a piece of paper from which he read in a thunderous voice: 'Here Daniel Defoe tells us: "The many dismal objects which happened everywhere as I went about the streets, had filled my mind with a great deal of horror for fear of the distemper, which was indeed very horrible in itself . . . the swellings, which were generally in the neck or groin, when they grew hard and would not break, grew so painful that it was equal to the most exquisite torture; and some, not able to bear the torment, threw themselves out at windows or shot themselves, or otherwise made themselves away . . . "

'And listen to this, brothers and sisters: "I could tell dismal stories of living infants being found sucking the breasts of their mothers, or nurses, after they have been dead of the plague . . . " '

'That's the reincarnation of Solomon Eagle,' said the American with the tape-recorder.

'Beg pardon, sir,' said the policeman.

'Solomon Eagle. He was some screwball prophet who ran naked through London with a pan of burning charcoal on his head, crying judgement on the city during the Great Plague. I've been reading up my Defoe, too.' He patted his tape-recorder. 'I'm from Global News.'

'Indeed, sir.'

The constable's transceiver crackled and he held it to his ear for a moment, then muttered something into the microphone.

'Excuse me, duty calls.' He began walking quickly towards the entrance of the Hyde Park underground car park. The man from Global reached into his gadget bag for a flashgun which he clipped on to his Pentax, and followed. He'd heard enough over the radio to know that a woman had been found dead in a parked car, her skin blackened.

With luck he'd get the first picture of the plague victim.

Two days later, in the long conference room overlooking the Thames, the Chief Medical Officer glanced round the semicircle of men and women who, as members of the GLC or heads of departments and city organisations, had assembled for their daily conference. With extra telephones installed, maps and blackboards on the walls, it had become the operational centre for dealing with the crisis. Beside Peter Barnet sat the Permanent Under-Secretary for Health who had been designated the link between the GLC and the Cabinet.

'I shall start with a very brief résumé of the situation, from the Health Department's viewpoint, since we last convened,' said Peter. 'Reports up until an hour ago put the total of plague deaths at over eight thousand.'

He gestured to a map of Greater London covering an entire wall. 'The black pins mark the homes of the deceased, the red pins represent cases which are still alive. Worst hit so far are the areas where the men who entered the plague pit resided . . . East Ham, Streatham, Camden Town and so on. Of the suburbs, Harrow and Pinner are the worst affected. However, it is obvious that within a week the pattern will be universal. What we see now is the result of the first wave of infection, and the incubation period heralding the second wave will soon be complete.'

'Has a projection been made for the likely deaths then?' said the blue-rinsed lady from the Social Services department. 'Surely you must appreciate our need to plan ahead. We'll need to get more Death Certificates printed and . . . ' She was an old political enemy of the Chief Medical Officer, and her tone contained all the antagonism which had been bred during the bitter days of the Government-imposed cutbacks.

'As to a projection, your guess is as good as mine,' said Peter Barnet wearily. He turned to one of his advisers. 'Have you any idea, Walter?'

'The real outbreak came on Christmas Eve with five hundred reported cases – that doubled on Christmas Day, and next day doubled again. If that continues to be the trend you can work it out for yourself – by the end of the first week there will be over thirty thousand victims.'

'Meanwhile, our inoculation teams have been working round the clock,' said Peter Barnet. 'All GLC personnel, the police force, firemen, medical staff and members of the essential service industries – power, water and sewerage operatives – have been treated. The magnitude of this programme has depleted our stocks of serum, and until more arrives we cannot inaugurate a programme of immunisation for the general public. Unfortunately several countries holding large stocks of Haffkine vaccine have gone back on their promise of aid in case the infection should spread to their shores . . . ' He gave a bitter smile. 'As usual the Americans have proved the most generous, but the fact remains that until the production of serum catches up with the demand the best we can do is use antibiotics on people once the infection has been diagnosed . . . '

'Is it true that large amounts of serum have been diverted to inoculate the armed forces outside London?' demanded the lady from Social Services.

'Correct,' said the Under-Secretary. 'The probability is that we'll soon be needing them in London as society starts to break down.'

'Surely the police . . . '

The Commissioner of Police looked stony-faced and said, 'Perhaps the Under-Secretary could explain further . . . '

'Yes, the objective of the Government is to prevent the spread of plague to the rest of the country. Already motorways have been sealed off, and train services in and out of London shut down apart from special goods trains bringing in food. On recommendation from the World Health Organisation – coupled with the fact that all overseas airlines have cancelled in-bound flights – Heathrow Airport will be closed for the duration of the epidemic. However, to isolate the city completely it may be necessary to cordon it off – road blocks, patrols of open ground beyond the suburbs and so on.'

There was a gasp as his listeners realised the meaning of

his words, then everyone began talking at once. As the outraged hubbub died the Council Chairman rose with ominous dignity.

'I am aware that in the Great Plague of 1665 attempts were made to seal off the city,' he said. 'There were special toll-gates erected and only those with certificates of health, signed by what I believe were known as chirurgeons, were allowed to pass beyond city limits. But in those days London was still partly walled, its population was less that a twentieth of what it is today, and it would be madness in the twentieth century to attempt to cordon off a city so huge and complex . . . '

They were his last words.

For a millisecond the conference room was filled with searing orange light, then the shock wave of the explosion rocked the building. Windows disintegrated into glass shards which sliced through the assembly like fragments from a mortar shell. The wall curved inwards in an almost graceful wave of masonry.

Peter Barnet lay against the wall where the blast had hurled him. It was a long moment before he could take in what had happened, a long moment of shocked silence before the screaming began. Through the jagged gap in the outside wall most of the bright sky had been blotted out by a billowing cloud of oily smoke, its underside tinged with flame. The conference room as such had disappeared. There was an expanse of floor littered with bodies, some beginning to move in agony, others mere blood-soaked bundles. The Under-Secretary, his face gashed where the flying splinters had caught him, helped Peter to his feet.

'Must have been a bomb,' he said. 'At such a time . . . Come on, man, people need help . . . '

But Peter made no response. He just gazed at a head which lay open-eyed and open-mouthed at his feet, and by its blue hair he knew that it was his old antagonist from Social Services.

'Pilot Error' was the nearest the inquiry got to pinpointing the cause of the crash of Flight BA101 from Zurich. Tapes from Air Traffic Control indicated that all was well up to two minutes before the 727 should have made the last landing permitted at Heathrow. Then there had been a brief babel of sounds which made even the hardened investigators wince.

One eye-witness, miraculously located in the confused days which followed, described how the aircraft had plummeted out of the sky, then seemed to pull out and skim the surface of the Thames as though attempting to belly-land before exploding against Westminster Bridge.

There had been no commercial passengers aboard, the BA101 being on a return flight carrying the bulk of the anti-plague serum held by the Red Cross at its Swiss headquarters. Ironically the autopsy on the body of the captain, which was retrieved by frogmen, showed a septicaemic condition caused by plague bacilli.

10

It has just been announced at Buckingham Palace that it is the intention of King Charles to remain in the capital. His Majesty is quoted as saying, 'We believe that this visitation is something we must see through together. Londoners cannot be expected to accept the quarantining of their city if they see me making a bolt for it. We believe that with God's help and our own good sense we will come through, just as our ancestors did.'

'Good old Charlie!' exclaimed Bud Schuster who, although a United States citizen, was an ardent royalist. He pulled up the Hertz car outside a shabby little pub, switched off the radio and looked about him. Like a lot of London streets these days it was empty, its gutters choked with sodden litter. Ahead of him a row of terraced houses awaiting demolition looked curiously blind with their window panes vandalised; opposite, brick warehouses and wholesalers' shops were equally deserted. At the corner a tobacconist's was boarded up with heavy planks, ideal for what Bud had in mind.

Slinging his Pentax over one shoulder, and his portable recorder over the other, he left the car and walked over to the abandoned shop. Taking a stick of red chalk from his pocket he drew a large cross on the planking, under which he inscribed in crude block letters LORD HAVE MERCY ON US.

Stepping back, he photographed his handiwork from several angles. Subtlety was not one of Bud's attributes, as everyone on the Global News Agency knew, but his hustling technique got results. His photograph of an actual plague victim had been the first to be wired out of London.

His camera-work completed, he walked into the Lord Nelson, where several elderly customers sat on benches against the flock-papered walls. He ordered a Scotch from the landlady.

'Cheers,' he said to an old man having his glass refilled with draught beer.

The old man nodded, and said, 'Fill 'er up, Hazel. It's the only way I know of taking it with me.'

'On me,' said Bud, hastily pushing a note across the bar.

'You're an American, ain't yer,' said the old man, surveying him with rheumy eyes. 'Reckon yer're a mug to stay in London at a time like this.'

Bud smiled confidently. He was in Paris when the plague story broke and before leaving he had visited the American Hospital where, as he put it, he had 'more stuff pumped in his ass than when he'd been assigned to Nam'. The limeys might drop all round him, but Bud Schuster was sacrosanct!'

'I'm a researcher for the United Nations,' he confided.

'That's nice,' said Hazel, wiping the dry bar by reflex action. 'Doing a survey, are you?'

Bud nodded.

'It started round here, yer know,' wheezed the old man. 'Them blokes were right here in this bar the day it happened.'

'Oh, Frank . . . ' Hazel remonstrated.

''Course nothing's been said about it official like,' he continued defiantly. 'You can see the place from here.'

'I hear a crypt was opened by mistake,' said Bud.

There was an uneasy silence. Hazel glared at her customers as though daring them to speak.

'Really, there was nothing in the papers or on the telly,' she said. 'Nobody never came to the pub about it. There's no infection here, I can tell you. Anyway, it's time for the news.' She turned on the television set above the glass cabinet imprisoning cold pork pies and crisp packets. While the customers gazed at images of the King, and aircraft wreckage being cleared from Westminster Bridge, Bud led the old man to a corner.

'I'm making a report on the outbreak,' he whispered confidentially. 'If you could show me where . . . ' He opened his billfold.

'I don't care what you're doin', I'll show you,' said the old man, unabashed as he thumbed his gnarled fingers in a time-honoured gesture.

Minutes later Bud stood in the middle of the building site where a few days earlier Hacker had gone berserk in his JCB.

'It's under that heap of rubble,' the old man said. 'There's been a GLC watchman sittin' in that little hut, but he ain't turned up today. Reckon they should've concreted it over, but they didn't want to draw folks' attention to it. Know what I mean. 'Course I always knew what it was. My family's lived here for generations, and we all knew.'

'That right?' said Bud.

'Course. Usta be fields here in the Great Plague days, and there were pits all over. Just imagine. 'Undreds of stiffs. It'll be like that again. Wonder where they'll put us this time?'

'Thanks, Frank. I'll take a closer look.'

'That's up to you,' said the old man. 'I ain't going an inch nearer. Ought to be concreted, but they don't give a stuff about us.'

He took the money the American handed him.

'Thank's mister,' he said. 'I can use this. I might not

make it to next pension day.' He laughed and coughed on his humour, then added inconsequently, 'When I was a youngster I used to drive a dray round here.'

He winked grotesquely, and walked away over the ground.

Alone on the site Bud photographed the pile of broken brickwork whose mortar remained intact despite the very dramatic, he thought. Need something better than this.

He circled to the mound.

Goddam it! It was worth a try!

Checking to make sure he was still unobserved, he began to lift bricks away. Sweat was soon trickling down his face, but he was delighted to find he could burrow under a slab of brickwork whose mortar remained intact despite the pounding of the JCB scoop. It had held loose bricks in position, but by removing some of them Bud was rewarded by suddenly finding himself staring into a black opening about a metre across. Was it his imagination or was there a mephitic taint to the air?

Full length on the rubble slope beneath the overhang, he lit a match and, setting fire to a crumpled letter from his ex-wife, let it flutter into the darkness.

In its flickering light bones and skulls materialised briefly out of the darkness.

The source!

He'd found the source of the Black Death which was going to decimate one of the great capitals of the world, and probably the rest of Britain. And it had all begun in this pit. It was an awesome thought.

He inched backwards until he was able to stand upright, checked to make sure that he was still unobserved, then clipped the flashlight to his camera. Once more he crawled beneath the slab of mortared brick until he had reached the edge of the hole. As he squirmed into position a loose brick tumbled past him and disappeared into the blackness.

Bud adjusted his camera's focussing and aperture rings to their optimum setting, then lowered his arm into the cavity and pressed the camera's shutter release. For a fraction of a second the pit was filled with electronic light, causing patterns to dance before his eyes after the darkness returned. The motordrive buzzed, he turned the camera to a new angle and pressed the release again, this time remembering to close his eyes. With the use of a wide-angled lens, he hoped he would get a percentage of acceptable pictures of the bone-scattered mould beneath the brick ceiling from which hung slender stalactites. Whether they were some repulsive fungoid growth or lime formations from the ancient cement he could not tell. But whatever they were, he was damn sure they would make the pictures look suitably eerie, reaching down towards skull and ribcage.

It reminded him of a story called *A Cask of Amontillado* which had scared the pants off him when he was a kid. Written by Edgar Allan Poe, it was about a character named Montresor who took his intoxicated enemy into a catacomb, pretending that he needed his advice on some choice sherry stored there, and then – among the litter of bones just as in this pit – he walled him up alive.

That story had given him nightmares. But since then he had seen the real horror of the world. What was some guy being bricked up compared with a napalmed village! You didn't need to be some sort of shrink to know that people got over their real fears by turning them into fantasy, by reading horror novels or going to horror movies.

Well, this was the real thing. Tomorrow millions would see a real view of hell through his pictures.

To get a better angle he needed to lower the Pentax. He wriggled forward cautiously, then felt the bricks beneath him begin to move. In trying to crawl backwards more bricks were dislodged. He fell amidst an avalanche of rubble through the gap to hit the soft mould with an impact that sent the breath hissing from his lungs. Debris rained down on him painfully and it seemed that the jagged circle of daylight above him went out.

For a minute he lay dazed, then in a terrible darkness the truth of what had happened struck him. The shifting of the bricks had caused the slab to slide and seal the entrance.

Bud Schuster was tough. He'd had to be to survive so long in the service of Global. And now he did not panic. He fumbled for his matches and struck one. As it fizzed into life he started back as he saw the empty sockets of a skull glaring at him, the mouth – with half its teeth missing – within several inches of his own.

With an oath he rose to a kneeling position and gazed at the masonry above until the match seared his thumb. It would be a matter of keeping his cool. In his pocket he had an *A-Z of London*. By burning a page at a time he would have light for a while, certainly enough to begin digging himself out.

As a page detailing the outer reaches of Barnet flared, he pressed against the slab, and his first hint of fear came with the realisation he could not budge it an inch. Perhaps there was some other part of the roof that he could tunnel through. While the spills made from rolled up atlas pages cast a wavering pool of light, he crawled across the bone-strewn surface as the site-clearing gang had done in their search for treasure. But by the time his matches were running low he had seen enough to know there was no way he could claw his way to freedom.

All he could do was wait. That old guy would raise the alarm when he saw that his car remained outside the Lord Nelson. Meanwhile he may as well use up his film. It was only when the reel came to an end, when there was nothing to do but wait, that unease began to replace his confidence. It reminded him too much of another Poe story which had also made him shudder as a kid. It was *Premature Burial*!

For what seemed an age he hunched in the dark, telling himself it was a matter of relaxing until help came. When he decided that an hour must have passed he pressed the button to illuminate the face of his Seiko watch. To his amazement only twenty minutes had gone by.

He moved and, in reaching out, felt the skeletal hand of a child which had lain there for three centuries. The contact made his heart thud – he was sure he could hear it! – and in the silence of the grave he was aware of the blood pulsing through his arteries, of the noise his throat made when he swallowed, of his breathing which was becoming more rapid.

And there was something else. He was sure there was something else. Rats? No, it was not so much a scrabbling . . . more a whisper . . . But what could whisper in this place of the dead?

The control he had kept on himself up to this moment snapped. With prayers and curses he began to scrabble at the brickwork above his head until warm blood trickled down his wrists, and the horrors of Edgar Allan Poe mocked him from the ultimate darkness.

'Please God, let him live. Please God, let him live.'

At the words Paul opened his eyes. His body was too hot and the searing in his left side grew as consciousness returned until he had to bite back a scream of agony. When the tide of pain receded he was aware of the haggard face of Charity above his, with salty lines on her cheeks where tears had coursed.

'Oh darling. I've been trying to get help. When I finally got through on the number I was put on a list, and no one has come.'

For a moment he was unable to speak. His tongue was so clumsy in his mouth, it felt twice its normal size.

'I'm sorry,' he managed faintly. 'I think I've . . . the bed feels wet . . . '

'You've been sweating while you were asleep. I'll change the sheets now you're awake. Would you like a drink first?'

He nodded feebly.

She retreated out of his range of vision, returning moments later with a teapot. Placing the spout between his lips, she carefully poured a small amount of water into his mouth. As it moistened the dry membrane he tried to form words again.

'How long . . . was I out?'

'I don't know.' She glanced at her watch. 'Ten hours, something like that.'

'How about you?'

'All right so far.' She tried to joke. 'Maybe the bugs don't like brown blood . . . '

In his aberrated mental state this struck him as hilarious.

He laughed hysterically, but the laughter turned to a coughing fit and Charity wiped away blood-tinged froth with paper torn from a kitchen roll.

Exhausted, he lay still and she gave him more water. As he swallowed he momentarily regained control.

'It's three days since I went down?'

She nodded.

'It figures,' he gasped.

'I've kept up the injections.'

'You've been amazing. You must be exhausted.'

'I set the alarm. Feel like some soup? I got dozens of Campbell's Cream of Chicken from poor Mrs Patel.'

'Just water. What's been happening in the outside world?'

'I don't really know. Everything seems to be falling apart from the bits I've heard on the radio . . . Oh darling, what's the matter?'

The terrible throbbing had returned to his side. His chest rose and fell like a bellows as he fought for air.

'Help me. For God's sake, help me.'

Seeing he was clutching himself below his left armpit, Charity pulled back the blanket and for a moment felt she was going to faint. The fingers of his right hand were spread over a huge purplish swelling, a swelling which looked as though there was a cricket ball implanted beneath his skin.

As the spasms eased he managed to speak again.

'The antibiotic doesn't seem to have prevented the bulbo from forming. Maybe I've got antibiotic resistance . . . '

The tide of pain flowed back, doubling up his body and this time it was so bad that he could not prevent himself screaming.

'A knife . . . get me a knife,' he shouted. 'Be quick!'

For a moment Charity believed that he wanted to commit suicide, then she knew what had to be done. She ran to the kitchen and from a drawer took out a small sharp-pointed Sabatier knife.

'Give it to me,' he moaned and held out his hand, but it was shaking so badly she ignored it.

'Lie still, darling,' she said. 'Take your hand away.'

Perhaps he could not hear her, or perhaps he had lost

control of his body which was now rolling from side to side. It was pure instinct which guided her. She drew back her left hand and, with all her strength, struck him across his stubbled face. For a moment the shock made him go rigid and he half raised his hands as though to protect himself from another blow. And at that moment she pressed with her right hand, the point of the knife slicing into the stretched skin, then stopping as it encountered the hardness of the infected lymphatic gland. With Paul's agony ringing in her ears, she grasped her wrist with her left hand and leaned forward with all her weight.

She felt the blade part the hard tissue and slide into the swelling. Something hot splashed over her fingers. The stench which filled her nostrils made her retch and, turning away, she wrenched out the knife. She reeled back across the room and collapsed into a chair, lowering her head to try and overcome her nausea.

When Charity steeled herself to look at Paul's side, a large patch of the bed was covered with yellow viscid fluid, but the ghastly swelling had shrunk unbelievably. From the slit she had made clear blood was oozing.

As she pressed one of her treasured damask table napkins against the wound, she saw his face was frozen in a rictus which made her believe his death was close.

Raymond Carson sat alone in the Radio City newsroom, an open bottle of beer on his desk and a telephone clamped to his ear. Empty bottles filled his waste bin while several full crates were piled up in a corner. Come hell or high water – or plague! – he had sworn, he was not going to allow himself to run short of essential supplies.

White stubble covered his normally ruddy features, his greying hair fell in greasy wisps over his forehead and his shirt smelled of stale sweat. He hadn't changed it since the 747 had crashed three days ago. During that time he had remained at the news desk, snatching brief naps on the rest-room sofa during the early hours when the agency teleprinter reduced its endless chatter to spasmodic outbursts. As several members of the staff had not reported for work – two were known to have died of the plague – it was

Vic Kelly's decision to work with as few personnel as possible on the premises to reduce the risk of infection. Raymond's staff avoided the office, phoning in their stories, while Phil Jason and a single engineer kept the station on air.

'Have you got a line on that black market serum yet?' Raymond demanded. 'I know it's impossible to get a quote from Scotland Yard – they've got enough on their hands right now without worrying about black marketeers. That's right – try and buy some and then get in analysed – it's probably only coloured water. For once I don't give a damn about expenses. Yeah, and try and find where they have got the bottle labels and packaging from. We're doing a public warning on it tonight, and I want to tie in with Joe's story on raids on chemists' shops for antibiotics. Keep healthy!'

He rang off and looked up as Tim Holt came in, followed by an old man whose snowy beard was marred by a nicotine stain at the side of his mouth.

'Ray, I'm delighted to say we've got hold of Sir Robert McAusland. He's agreed to do a phone-in with Phil on what to do until the doctor comes.'

He grinned weakly at his little joke. Unlike the news editor, he had managed to remain remarkably spruce through shaving regularly and changing his clothes from the private wardrobe in his office. Typically he was the only man at Radio City who could still have passed as an executive.

'Very good of you to come along, sir,' said Raymond automatically. 'Our listeners could do with some re-assurance. Know the latest score?'

'Officially it's fifty thousand,' said Sir Robert, 'but that's only based on hospital reports and bodies found and disposed of. It's probably twice that number, with people lying dead in their houses and bedsits. The city is just starting to smell. Mind you, it's nothing yet . . . '

'How about the rest of the country?'

'I've no information. The Research Unit of the Royal College of General Practitioners at Birmingham, which monitors GPs throughout the country, has not reported any cases . . . yet.'

The old man brought out his tobacco and began to roll a cigarette.

'I'm a doctor of the old school,' he explained. 'I still think tobacco is an excellent prophylactic.'

'Talking about that, I've got a story here that all the camphor in London has been sold out,' said Raymond. 'Apparently there's an old wives' tale going round that it'll prevent infection.'

'That takes me back to the old infantile paralysis outbreaks,' said Sir Robert. 'Mothers used to hang it round their kids' necks in little bags. But I suppose it's as effective as anything else we've got at the moment.'

The news editor looked up quickly, his sixth sense stirring.

'Surely the serum, when we get enough . . . '

Sir Robert smiled enigmatically.

'The present epidemic was caused by viral organisms from the Great Plague of London. The serums we're using are cultured from present-day strains, don't you see?'

'No.'

Tim Holt glanced up at the large clock with its remorseless sweep hand.

'Time to go to the studio, Sir Robert,' he said.

'I'd like to ask a favour,' said the old man. 'You have a programme called *Lifeline* to help people trace each other, don't you?'

'Yes, we've had to extend it to three hours each evening,' said the programme manager with a touch of pride. 'The Beeb has taken over the idea – as usual!'

'There's a man I'm desperately anxious to contact,' said Sir Robert. 'Perhaps you could put out a call . . . '

'Give me the details after the phone-in,' said Tim, his eye on the clock. 'This way, Sir Robert.'

When he had gone Raymond Carson looked thoughtful. In the corner of the room the teleprinter began to spew out words on its endless roll. Probably the Financial Times Index had gone through the floor . . .

He picked up the receiver and pressed a sequence of well-remembered numbers.

For a long minute he listened to the distant berp-berp, his heart suddenly beating faster than usual. Then a woman said cautiously, 'Hello?'

'Connie . . . '

'Who is that?'

'It's me.'

'Who?'

'Me. Bloody hell, don't you remember what I sound like! It's Ray . . . '

'What do you want?'

'Well, I . . . I was concerned about you . . . are you all right? Is there anything I can do? I mean, with the plague and everything, I just wanted to get in touch . . . '

'That's rather pointless, Raymond. I've nothing to say to you.' She rang off.

With a sigh the news editor flipped the cap off a bottle.

'Life's a bastard,' he said aloud.

11

You are listening to Radio City – your lifeline station – and here is Newsflash. *As the death toll mounts hourly, from Edinburgh the Home Secretary announced further steps to confine the contagion to the capital. Road blocks, manned by Armed Services personnel, have now been set up on all routes leading out of Greater London. Foot and helicopter patrols are keeping surveillance on open ground to intercept refugees.*

As from now it is illegal to leave the limits of Greater London unless you are on essential business and can produce an official certificate of health. In order to minimise the spread of infection within the city, regulations have been confirmed making it illegal for pubs and places of entertainment to admit the public. Shops, apart from those supplying food – and chemists – are also to close.

To implement these measures Martial Law has been proclaimed and extra troops are being flown in from Ulster and West Germany. Armed military patrols are already operating in London to prevent looting and acts of violence.

Meanwhile it is not only London which has become isolated: within the city itself several no-go areas have been established. In Southall barricades were erected following what the Asian Peoples' Community Council describe as extreme provocation from the New Britain Party which alleges that plague was introduced by immigrants. A similar no-go area has been declared in Brixton . . .

The stutter of a distant drum drew Charity to the window. At the end of the square she saw Union Jacks rippling above a column of marching men. From the distance it seemed as though they were wearing some sort of uniform and she realised members of the New Britain Party were parading for the benefit of the cosmopolitan population of Notting Hill Gate.

She shrugged. What did it matter? None of them might be alive in a week's time. *Pasteurella pestis* was the ultimate democrat: it paid no heed to skin colouring, religious belief or political spectrum. It did not matter whether the host believed in Marx or Christ – once the bacilli entered his bloodstream the plague mark would appear just the same and soon he would be dead.

She returned to the bedroom where Paul Mitchell lay like an effigy on her bed. From being cyanosed, his features had changed to waxy white, his breath was shallow and he no longer twitched in his sleep as though tormented by some inner hallucination. She took his pulse. It was certainly slower and she was afraid that he was slipping away from her.

She sponged his forehead and then went again to the telephone, although she knew she would be answered by a pre-recorded voice.

'This is your emergency health centre,' the pre-recorded voice announced. 'If you are in need of medical help please speak your name, address and symptoms clearly at the end of this message and all cases will be dealt with in strict rotation. If a member of your family has become deceased please dial your operator and you will be connected with your local disposal service. In the meantime avoid contact with the dead or their clothing and soiled bed linen . . . '

Charity hung up.

It seemed she had heard this voice a hundred times, and each time she had left her message, but no help arrived. From what she knew of the virulence of the plague it was unlikely there were enough doctors or health workers left to cope with a fraction of those needing their care.

It was strange that she had not been affected, though Paul had explained that some people possessed a natural immunity. Believing that in an earlier incarnation she had perished in one of the Seven Plagues of Egypt, she decided that destiny was sparing her this form of death in her present life.

She wondered if, in some future life, she and Paul would be reunited. Was there an affinity between souls which brought them together time after time in this curious phenomenon called life? She had thought about it constantly as she had sat by his bed. She loved him so much, and such an intense love could not have developed just in the few horrendous days she had known him. There must be some deeper link between them.

An alarm clock trilled. Time for his injection.

At that moment there was a heavy knock at the door which made her heart leap. In the beginning she had feared such a sound in case it was the police coming to arrest him – which was why she had ignored the telephone – but now it could mean help was on hand at last. She turned the bolt and released the chain, hoping to see a white-coated doctor or ambulance men with a stretcher.

Instead she saw a stranger, a wild-looking man with tangled hair down to his shoulders and a carving knife in his hand. Without a word he pressed the point between her breasts so that she was forced to back into the hallway.

The sergeant scowled behind his anti-contamination mask as he surveyed the canvas-topped army truck from which he had just alighted. On the grime-covered side someone had scrawled BRING OUT YOUR DEAD.

'Trooper Hoddle, get them words removed,' he shouted through the chemical-impregnated filter. 'They're in shocking bad taste.'

'Sir,' said the young soldier who, like the sergeant, was dressed in a silvered suit designed to protect troops against a germ-warfare attack. While the trooper wiped the side of the truck, the sergeant looked at the clipboard in his gloved hands.

'The Lord Nelson,' he said wearily. 'Right lad, in we go.' The private followed him reluctantly into the bar where a dozen old men and women were seated on benches, glasses of spirits and pints of bitter in their hands.

'Blimey, you look like you're out of *Doctor Who*,' chuckled an old man with rheumy eyes who was refilling his tankard from a beer pump. 'Or is it *Star Wars*?'

His joke was greeted by a ripple of laughter and coughing from the customers. An obese woman toasted him with her glass of port and lemon, and began singing 'Now is the Hour' which caused even more painful hilarity.

'Where is the deceased?' the sergeant demanded.

The old man pointed to the other side of the bar.

'If you mean Hazel, she's down there,' he said. 'She just dropped so I rang the number like they told us on the radio.'

'If you ask me she's just pissed,' said the lady with the port and lemon. 'She put it away on the quiet, did Hazel.' She leaned over the bar. 'Mind you, she hasn't moved all day.' She burst into tipsy laughter. 'Will you look at them pink knickers . . .'

'Right, Trooper, you know the drill,' said the sergeant, ignoring invitations to take off his *Flash Gordon* suit and have a drink.

'Everything's on the house today,' explained the old man unnecessarily.

Behind the bar the young soldier bent over Hazel and gently tidied her skirt, then raised her so the sergeant could draw on a plastic body bag.

Between them they lifted the black form and carried it

out of the pub where a silence had fallen as for a moment the reality of death penetrated alcoholic euphoria. Then the fat woman began singing 'Now is the Hour' again and the party resumed. Outside, the two men heaved the corpse over the tailboard where it came to rest among similar sealed bundles. The trooper dropped the canvas curtain while the sergeant took up his clipboard to read their next destination.

'She ain't the only one around here,' said the rheumy old man who had followed them out with his pint in his shaking hand.

'What do you mean?'

He pointed to a parked car.

'A yank came yesterday. Tried to tell me some cock and bull story about working for the United Nations . . . ' He chuckled. 'But I could see he was a reporter. So I took him to the pit, and he ain't come back by the look of things.'

'I suppose we'd better take a look,' said the sergeant.

'Excuse me, sir, but shouldn't we empty the pub first,' said the soldier. 'According to regulations they're supposed to be closed down.'

'True, it's against regulations, but seeing that the landlady is deceased and no money is being passed over the counter, one might say that it's no longer a pub – rather a private party. Shall we let the poor old sods have their last day on the house?'

'Of course, sir.'

'Right, let's go and find the American. It may save us having to come back later.'

The two soldiers followed the old man to the demolition site where he pointed to the distant pile of rubble.

'That's what interested him,' he explained. 'The pit is underneath that lot.'

The men surveyed the mound covering the pit. Suddenly, from beneath it came a sound which made all three back away. It was laughter. Low, chuckling, anile laughter.

The old man was the first to recover, delighted that the subterranean noise had proved his words.

'He's still down there,' he said. 'Just fancy that, been down there all this time.'

The soldiers approached the debris. Together they heaved at the heavy slab which acted as a capstone, but were unable to lift it.

'Need earth-moving equipment,' muttered the sergeant, his transparent mask misting up with his heavy breathing.

'Perhaps I can shift these bricks under it,' said Trooper Hoddle, kneeling down and delving into the shattered bricks with his hands. As he did so the laughter floating out of the earth was replaced with a keening sound that made him dig with a new urgency.

After a few minutes several bricks dropped inwards to reveal a small black hole.

'You down there,' shouted the sergeant. 'Are you hurt?'

In the aperture appeared a hand from which the skin hung in strips and whose nails had been torn away. It rose into the air as though it were an entity on its own, then withdrew into the darkness to be replaced by a face which even the sergeant was to remember in his nightmares. Once it had been human, but now it was only the vestigial mask of a man. Terror had turned the eyes to those of a lunatic, the straggling hair hanging over the grimed forehead had become a dirty white, the mouth was a slit in a patch of clotted blood where the victim had bitten through his lips. Beneath the eyes nerves twitched continuously.

'What'll we do?' muttered the trooper. 'I can't make the hole any wider.'

The terrible face vanished as though the daylight had been too much for it and the chuckling resumed.

'Trooper, you will go back to the truck and from the driver there collect one carbine which you will bring back here,' said the sergeant. 'As fast as you can, lad.'

Trooper Hoddle was back within a minute with the gun.

'Ahoy down there,' called the sergeant. 'Show yourself.' He lowered his voice and added, 'Trooper, fire when I give the word.'

The carbine trembled in the young man's hands.

'Sir . . . I can't,' he said. 'Not in cold blood.'

'You are disobeying an order,' said the sergeant.

The trooper nodded.

'I know, sir, but that's how it is.'

'All right, Trooper. It's not as though we were at war. Give it to me.'

Gratefully he passed the weapon to the sergeant.

The laughter which seemed to rise like an invisible column from the cavity ceased and the crazy face reappeared. As the trooper and the old man watched in shocked fascination, the blood-caked mouth opened and a voice which seemed to embody all the fear and agony of the world cried out, 'For the love of God, Montresor.'

The sergeant raised the carbine.

'If it's money you want . . .' Charity said backing from the knife until she felt her shoulders pressing against the wall. But the stranger shook his head, a string of saliva hanging from his slack mouth.

'Food. You need food?'

The man looked as though he had been sleeping rough, and there was mud down one side of his tartan lumber jacket.

Again he shook his head.

'Then what . . . ?'

He seemed impatient at her words. He looked about suspiciously, then his eyes returned to her and he grinned wolfishly, and all the time she felt the pressure of the blade against her skin.

Still he said nothing. They stood like some tableau in the hall and it occurred to her that she was faced by a madman. Up until this moment she had not felt fear, only outrage that her world should be invaded by force – the fear came when she glanced down and saw that his heavy work-boots were spotted with blood.

With his left hand he pulled open his jacket and the corduroy shirt beneath it, displaying a rash of purple spots, each the size of a five-pence piece, across his stomach.

'Sick!' he said, and sniggered.

Charity could think of no words.

'Kiss,' he said. Moving the knife with his right hand so that the point was against her fast-beating heart, he slid his left arm round her neck and before she realized what he intended he pulled her head towards him. His open mouth closed on hers and she felt his scalding tongue on her lips as he moved his head from side to side.

Her instinct was to struggle free, but the steady pressure of the knife held her paralysed while he continued in his attempt to prise open her lips. In her weakened state Charity felt a darkness veiling her eyes. Her only thought was to keep her teeth clamped together, to resist and preserve some particle of dignity despite the fact that he could easily kill her.

The darkness thickened, her knees trembled and she began to slide downwards with her assailant bending over her. Charity fought the nausea and opened her eyes, and what she saw over his shoulder sent a surge of hope through her. Next instant a large fleshy hand closed on her attacker's neck while the other twisted his wrist so hard the knife fell and embedded itself neatly in the parquet floor.

'Digger!' cried Charity.

Without a word the tall Australian whirled the intruder round and rushed him out on to the landing where his wail of protest was followed by a series of thuds as he was sent careering down the stairs.

While a murderous Vic Kelly followed the intruder to make sure he quit the building, the old man who had been with him entered the flat and, taking Charity kindly by the arm, said with a gentle Scottish accent, 'Take me to the bathroom, my dear, we must disinfect you. You can have hysterics after that if you like, but first things first.'

'No hysterics,' Charity muttered, grinding the back of her hand against her mouth.

'Allow me to do that,' said the old man. 'I used to practise medicine . . . ' He held up a black bag of the sort doctors carried years ago 'I've got just the stuff to take care of the problem . . . '

Charity sat on the edge of the bath while he swabbed her face with a bitter antiseptic and then sprayed her mouth and throat with an antibiotic aerosol.

'Now I'm going to give you an injection to be on the safe side,' he said, taking a disposable syringe from a plastic container. 'I think I'd better give your Aussie friend one, too, when he gets back. My name's McAusland, by the way. That's it, just roll up your sleeve.'

'I don't go much on your taste in boyfriends, sweetheart,' said Vic Kelly, entering the flat. 'I should've thought a Sheila with your class could've done better for herself . . . '

'I never thought I'd be speaking to you again, Digger,' said Charity. 'But thanks for turning up like you did. I still don't really understand . . . '

'I can tell you that an epidemic of these proportions brings out the best and the worst of human nature, and I speak from experience,' said Sir Robert. 'Some people will give up their lives trying to help others – others will plunder the dying. What happened just now was one of the worst manifestations of the human psyche under stress – and it's nothing new. Read Bell on the Great Plague of London and you'll find it mentioned there.'

'I'm not sure that I follow you.'

'It's a desire that comes about in certain individuals who, knowing that their hours are numbered, get a perverted revenge against their fate by passing on the contagion. A man dying of the plague will seize a woman in the street – or in your case, in her home – and kiss her to infect her. Cases have been known of infected women breathing into the mouths of babies . . . '

'I don't think I want to hear any more,' Charity said with a shudder. 'Please come and do something for Paul. He's in a very bad way.'

When Sir Robert entered the bedroom and saw the still body on the bed he exclaimed, 'Not as bad as you fear, my dear. As they used to say in Victorian melodramas, the crisis is over . . . '

'I was scared I'd done him harm.' And Charity found herself describing how she had lanced the swelling.

'I can tell you that without your efforts he would have been dead now. How do you think he became so badly infected while you have remained immune?'

'It was my fault, and I have not been able to get it out of my mind since he became ill. At his laboratory I spilled the specimen he had taken from a body at St John's Fever Hospital. He pushed me out of the cubicle, but . . . '

'But the bacilli got to him,' Sir Robert concluded. 'So he got the infection straight from an original victim. Very interesting. Now Mr Kelly, I suggest you go down to that posh car of yours and radio for an ambulance to get this gentleman to the clinic. I don't think, Miss Brown, you realise how important he is, or how hard I have been trying to find him. When I was at Radio City it was Mr Kelly who suggested that you'd be together, and though he'd telephoned you several times to no avail, I persuaded him to drive me here in the hope of finding some clue to your whereabouts.'

Charity gave Vic a hostile glare.

'If it hadn't been for Mr Kelly in the first place we wouldn't have had to go through all this . . . '

'Charity, it's no good coming the old acid with me now,' said The Digger. 'I'll whistle up help for your boyfriend and then you've got to listen to me whether you like it or not.'

Escorted by a military Land Rover, the ambulance arrived soon afterwards.

'What are the soldiers for?' demanded Charity as Paul's stretcher was lifted inside. 'Surely he's not being arrested again?'

'Of course not,' said Sir Robert. 'All ambulances are given protection now. A rumour spread that they carry anti-plague drugs and they are frequently hijacked. Or sometimes the mob will attack them for the hell of it. I shall travel with Paul to the clinic, and Mr Kelly can bring you to visit him. Goodbye for the moment, my dear.'

The old man climbed into the ambulance. The silver-suited driver of the armoured Land Rover gunned his engine and the two vehicles moved away with their warning lights flashing.

'C'mon, girl,' said Vic Kelly, opening the door of his Rolls Royce on which the silver fairy mascot had been replaced by a golden kangaroo. 'There's some hard yakka ahead for both of us.'

'Vic, I sometimes wonder if you're real,' said Charity.

'Yeah? I can tell you that under this rugged exterior . . . I'm as rough as guts.'

Charity was not amused.

'Okay, let's be serious. Thanks to me your professor will be as right as rain in the Alexander Memorial Clinic. They've got guards there – the lot. So in return you could at least get in and listen to me.'

Charity climbed into the back of the Rolls with The Digger.

'Ludgate Circus, sport,' he said to the chauffeur. 'And you'll be singing soprano if you scratch the paintwork on the wrecks.'

Charity saw what he meant as they turned out of Ladbroke Square into Kensington Park Road. On either side there were burnt-out cars and vans – sometimes the street was almost blocked by them and the Rolls inched between the gaps which had been forced by Army bulldozers.

'While you've been out of circulation rioting has become a popular pastime for the youth of this town,' Vic said. 'The "I'll-have-a-bit-of-fun-before-I-go" syndrome. Now, Charity, I admit I tipped off the Beeb that it might be an idea to vet your show before it went out, but I had no idea that you and Mitchell would be carted off by the johns. I know how you must feel towards me about it, but that can't be helped. As far as I'm concerned you're still on the Radio City payroll, and I want you to do a very special programme.'

He went on to explain how each day a syndicated feature was put together by what was left of the staff, but what he had in mind was something much bigger.

'I want you to fly over the city in a whirly-bird and describe it. I want you to make a classic human interest documentary that they'll be using in history classes a hundred years from now. So far we've pumped out routine stuff but I want the world to know what it's like to be caught up in the Second Great Plague of London, to have the stink of death up your nostrils, to step over a corpse with no more concern than you'd have in avoiding a dog turd, to feel sheer bloody terror each time you drop your pants in case the mark is on you . . .'

'I think I've got the picture,' said Charity coldly, but her professional interest was awakening.

For some minutes The Digger slumped back in moody silence. Faint rifle shots echoed from a long way off.

'Looters,' he said.

'When would you want me to get this on air?'

'The new motto of the company is "It's later than you think". I could arrange the hook-up for tomorrow.'

'Does the seat on the board still stand?'

The Digger roared with laughter.

'You make my illustrious ancestor Ned look like an amateur. Okay, Princess, I guarantee your seat on the board – the only thing I can't guarantee is that there'll be a board to have a seat on by next week.'

12

You have been listening to a selection of Georg Philipp Telemann's Trio Sonatas, and now for the news . . . The Foreign Secretary has confirmed that Britain has been virtually quarantined by the rest of the world following reports that plague had spread beyond Greater London. European and American airports have announced that there will be no landing facilities for British aircraft and British shipping has been warned to stay out of territorial waters by most maritime countries.

European dockers' unions have brought ferry services to a standstill and France has announced that naval vessels are patrolling the Channel to prevent people fleeing to the Continent in private boats.

At home, more cases of plague have been reported in Newcastle and Glasgow, both cities having Underground systems which are to be closed in line with London's anti-contagion precautions.

Abroad again. In Washington President Reagan has an-

nounced plans for massive financial aid to be made available to Britain for rehabilitation programmes. This has been criticised in Moscow as having political connotations at a time when Britain is likely to quit NATO . . .

The Westland Lynx army helicopter followed the course of the Thames at an altitude of five hundred metres. Reflecting the winter sun, the river wriggled like a slender silver snake through the city. Above Kew, Charity adjusted the throat microphone which would enable her to broadcast without interference from the helicopter's Rolls Royce engines. The pilot grinned at her appreciatively as she began the broadcast which was to make her internationally famous. Aware of the millions of people outside Britain who would be listening, she fought to control a nervous tremor in her voice as she introduced herself and described the vast city rolling towards the hazy horizon.

'Three hundred and twenty years ago this city suffered from the Great Plague when one sixth of its population was taken by dead carts and thrown into mass graves,' she continued. 'Less than a month ago the Black Death re-emerged from one of these pits and once again Londoners are being decimated by this invisible invader. Ironically, in this latter end of the twentieth century, when smallpox has been eradicated from the world and heart transplants no longer make headlines, this second plague is more of a nightmare than the first.

'At this height it would be hard to tell that there was anything amiss except for the smoke. Before the plague struck London, fire services dealt with scores of fires daily, but manpower has been so seriously depleted there are no longer enough fire crews to cope with all outbreaks. Major fires which are likely to spread are given priority, but as I look around the suburbs grey smudges indicate where detached houses have caught alight and have been left to burn themselves out.

'Such smudges are dwarfed by six columns of oily black smoke which dominate the city day and night. They rise from the communal pyres for London's dead. As I said, three centuries ago plague victims were collected by carts at night and dumped into huge pits, capable of holding hundreds of bodies before being covered over. Today the authorities have decided on communal cremation rather than communal burial. At open spaces in different parts of the city army trucks, acting as dead carts, arrive with loads of plastic-shrouded corpses to be piled in shallow trenches over which tanker-loads of petrol are pumped and then ignited. As we are now above Chiswick, the nearest of these billowing pillars rises from Wembley Football Stadium, once sacred to British football fans because it was here that the FA Cup was decided annually.

'Another difference between this visitation and the first is that in the Great Plague of London the dead carts only operated at night – today the ever-mounting number of deaths forces the army disposal service to operate round the clock. The grim statistics are that over half a million people have literally gone up in smoke above the city.'

Charity paused and in her earphone the engineer of Radio City assured her that she was coming through loud and clear.

'London's cremation fires can never be forgotten by those who see them,' she continued. 'It is an awesome manifestation of how nature can turn the tables on man, yet to me the most astonishing aspect of the last few days is how fast a city can regress to an almost medieval condition. The modern city has become too complex and sophisticated. In the Great Plague of London a householder was always able to draw water from a nearby well – today illness amongst the workforce needed to keep the metropolis supplied with water has meant that for days on end the supply does not reach certain areas. Water tankers, driven by courageous GLC staff, ensure that people have enough to drink, though they cannot wash or flush their lavatories.

'Someone once said that civilisation can be judged by the distance man puts between himself and his sewage. With the breakdown of water and electrical supplies to pumping stations, millions of Londoners are confronted by the problem of disposing of their own waste. The odour of excreta from open spaces and blocked sewers already permeates the city, and doctors fear a secondary epidemic of typhoid. By this yardstick alone our so-called civilisation is fading fast.

'Another aspect of the situation far worse than in the seventeenth century is the frightening upsurge of violence which ranges from muggings to full-scale riots. Here we are seeing the result of years of unemployment. There are thousands of Londoners in their early and mid-twenties who have never had an opportunity to work, or to believe that it is possible to improve their circumstances. They know there can be no prospect of things getting better for them even if they escape the epidemic, and their frustration erupts in violence for the sake of violence.

'A sense of responsibility is always bound up with a sense of future but people who have known nothing but the dole queue cannot see ahead. Their only outlet is to strike back at the society which they feel has cheated them of the right to express themselves through work or to earn enough to set up their own homes as their parents did before them. If a lesson has emerged for the rest of the world as a result of London's plague, it is this.

'But, while rioters take to the streets and looters brave army patrols to plunder the houses of the dead, there is the other side of the coin. Perhaps it is personified best by railwaymen who volunteered to bring the so-called "white trains" to London. With the city cordoned off from the rest of Britain, special freight trains shuttle in and out carrying essential supplies. Their drivers, who wear white decontamination suits which are sprayed with disinfectant each time they pass through medical checkpoints, work night and day to ensure that the problems of London are not added to by food shortages.

'Our helicopter is above the stretch of river between the Lambeth and Westminster Bridges, and I'm looking down directly on the deserted Houses of Parliament. To the west I can see a building equally well known to the tourists who used to visit London – Buckingham Palace – and the royal standard fluttering above it is perhaps the most heartwarming sight in London today. It means that the King has remained to face the crisis with his subjects.

'As our shadow flits across Westminster Abbey I imagine

I can hear bells, not only of this ancient place of worship but of other city churches, ringing for midday prayers. It was the suggestion of the Archbishop of Canterbury that at noon people of all denominations should unite in praying for deliverance. The idea was endorsed by His Holiness the Pope so that around the world Christians of many faiths and languages remember our plight at this hour.

'We are now swinging westward over what used to be the fashionable heart of the city. The streets below me are dotted with derelict vehicles and, perhaps on account of the petrol shortage, the only moving vehicles I can see are army patrols and a few ambulances escorted by motorcycle policemen.

'Park Lane with its luxury hotels has become a no-go area for the rich. Here, protected by private armies of masked security guards, those who can afford it have barricaded themselves against the plague rather as Prince Prospero did in the story of the *Red Death*. I am told that, apart from the astronomical price of staying in the Hilton or Dorchester, a condition is that each guest must be examined daily by resident doctors – and expelled at the first symptom of infection. Staff members are only admitted through the sandbagged entrances on production of health certificates.

'On several occasions over-stretched police and army personnel have been called to Park Lane to disperse demonstrators assembled in Hyde Park to protest violently against what they see as the privilege of wealth. But, although by nature a socialist, I cannot find it in my heart to condemn anyone who uses whatever means they have to avoid the agonising death which lurks in the very air about us.

'So far I have tried to describe the condition of the city but now I want to tell you what life is like for ordinary men and women – not teenage rioters, not sealed-off millionaires but the ordinary folk who have been confronted with a catastrophe no one believed could happen. Before coming on this flight I explored the streets in the area where I live. A few weeks ago they were bustling; now they are largely deserted. Most people only leave their homes to get food, for the rest of the time their only contact with the outside world is through radio and television. I will ask Radio City to play the tape I made during my wanderings this morning. When I return to you live I will be over the City of London, one of the great financial centres of the world which the Romans knew as Londinium . . .'

At Ludgate Circus an engineer switched over to Charity's tape which, even more than newsreels, brought home to the outside world the full meaning of the pestilence. Perhaps it was so effective because it was sound coverage. By listening to Charity's husky voice, by sharing her feelings expressed by an interjection or once by a gasp of horror, millions were able to imagine themselves in her place instead of spectators viewing a remote happening in between television commercials.

With her voice in their ears, accompanied by the tapping of her footsteps on the empty pavement, they could believe they were walking with her. In their minds they could picture the boarded-up shops, the litter blowing like tumbleweed down the streets, and the smell of the plague-stricken city – a nauseating combination of harsh disinfectant and the sweetish odour of decomposition.

Through her voice they saw the archetypal looter staggering down the street with a colour television, followed by a popping sound as an army patrol opened fire with rubber bullets. They followed her as, in her capacity as a reporter, she donned an anti-contamination suit and went into an old-fashioned terraced house with a disposal unit. With weary efficiency the men broke open a locked bedroom door and there in the bed lay an elderly couple like effigies on a medieval tomb. A half-empty bottle of tablets proclaimed that they had elected to die with dignity. This dignity was soon lost as, bagged in black plastic, they were carried from their life-long home to be finally separated in a jumble of bodies on the back of an army truck.

The next call was to a flat and here for the first time Charity found it difficult to continue. A mother, father and two children appeared to have died of the plague within hours of each other. It was only as the last body was being removed that a cry led Charity to a closed door behind which a one-year-old child, unaffected by the disease which had claimed its family, clutched a teddy bear in his cot.

The helicopter was hovering above the dome of St Paul's when Raymond Carson's voice sounded in Charity's headphones. 'The Digger wants you to keep going as long as you can,' he said. 'Seems half the world has come to a standstill to hear you. Remember you're speaking to some kid in New York with a transistor held to his ear and a family round a radio on a New Zealand sheep station. Probably your folk back in the Caribbean are listening right now, so give it everything you've got. Phil says your insert is coming to an end so here's the countdown to go live.'

For a moment, Charity closed her eyes as though summoning up strength to continue, then described a procession of pilgrims straggling up Ludgate Hill towards St Paul's behind a huge wooden cross.

Sir Robert McAusland sat on the edge of the bed and rolled one of his shapeless cigarettes.

'Well, Mitch, looks like you are one of the ten per cent who survive plague,' he said. 'I think you have your lady friend's knife-work to thank for that.'

Sitting in hospital pyjamas, Paul was a gaunt shadow of his former self. There were purple rings round his eyes and his fingers had a tendency to tremble. It was only his untidy fair hair and rimless glasses which gave a hint of his earlier boyish looks.

'Tell me, Mac,' he said, 'why did you come looking for me, and why am I in a VIP place like the Alexander Memorial?'

'I looked for you because I needed you. In fact you are the most needed man in this city which was why your treatment was given top priority. There's no need to look puzzled. I'm sure you must realise what I'm going to say.'

'Not entirely,' said Paul cautiously. 'But when I re-examined that *Pasteurella pestis* specimen there was something odd about it. I was bringing it down to show you on the night of the great exodus.'

Sir Robert nodded wearily.

'The problem is – and at the moment it's a very secret problem – the Haffkine vaccine is not preventing infection.'

'What?'

'It's true, I'm afraid. One may as well inoculate with distilled water for all the good it does.'

'That's unbelievable.'

'The plague bacilli does respond to antibiotic treatment so the only way to prevent its spread would be to put the entire population on a course of streptomycin or chlora-phenicol – which is impossible. Therefore we have to come up with an answer mighty fast. Inevitably cases are starting to appear outside London and if we don't have an effective serum soon what you're seeing here could sweep the rest of the British Isles and beyond. Apart from a nuclear holocaust I can't imagine a worse danger threatening mankind. And you have known me long enough to know that exaggeration is not one of my vices.'

'But why does the Haffkine fail?'

'It's very simple. The serums we have at our disposal are based on antigens made from killed bacilli.'

Paul nodded.

'That is straightforward enough. At first we were desperately short of the stuff but it was felt that once the vaccine labs around the world went into full production a nationwide inoculation scheme would be possible. Unfortunately those antigens are made from modern plague bacilli. The epidemic that we are suffering from is caused by seventeenth century bacilli, and I do not have to tell you of the genetic changes that can take place over such a period.

'Because of evolutionary progression, today's bacterium is a slightly different organism from that which existed in the time of Charles II. That difference is enough to make antigens derived from modern *Pasteurella pestis* ineffective. It's like influenza. We can never get an effective vaccine against it because once a decade we are under attack from the new strain.'

'That could explain the unusual bubonic symptoms associated with pneumonic infection,' said Paul, 'but it shouldn't be too difficult to come up with an answer.'

'It's a question of time,' Sir Robert said. 'At the moment the world has no protection against this form of plague which has remained dormant in a London plague pit. By the time a conventional serum has been developed, tested, put into mass production and distributed, millions of people will be dead. Somehow we have to short-circuit the process, and I think you are the man to do it.'

Paul did not look surprised at his words. 'Go on,' he said quietly.

'Laddie,' he said, 'when Miss Brown had you labelled Frankenstein in the popular media she was closer to the truth than she realised, wasn't she? Apart from developing long-stemmed rice and mould-resistant wheat, you *were* making monsters, weren't you? Tiny monsters that could only be seen with SEM equipment. Genetically engineered micro-organisms which, I seem to recollect, had the protection of the Official Secrets Act.'

'You seem rather well informed, Mac.'

'Of course. Ours is an incestuous little world and rumour spreads faster than in a girls' boarding school. I also understood that you had a disagreement with the panel set up to evaluate your results. Apparently they got cold feet when that Frankenstein nonsense was going on, and you were asked to stand down from the programme. Germ warfare, wasn't it?'

'In a sense,' Paul said slowly. 'I was approached to do a stint at Porton and I felt it was my patriotic duty to accept.'

'Patriotic duty?' mused Sir Robert. 'Those words have a rather old-fashioned ring about them, don't they? I didn't know that patriotism was compatible with microbiology.'

'In that case let me explain,' said Paul. 'It developed from an idea of mine that, through genetic engineering, mutant colonies of bacilli could be produced which were in effect cannibals. They would destroy their non-mutant brothers when they came into contact with them, and these traitor organisms could be introduced to their hosts through fine-droplet sprays.'

Sir Robert nodded.

'Of course. I read your paper on it in *Nature*. Naturally I was very interested. To an epidemologist like myself the idea was immensely attractive, particularly for Third World situations where aircraft fitted with atomisers could immunise a whole city in the space of an hour or two.'

'Exactly. And this system was to counter viral weapons a potential enemy might use against us. The problem was that, as we all know, such a potential enemy would not use a straightforward virus but an engineered strain against which we would have no antidote. Therefore, if I were to make mutants to counteract it, the first thing we would have to do would be to develop the same new strains our opposite numbers were likely to produce. The difference was that our research into improved versions of anthrax or cholera was purely for self defence.'

'Oh dear,' said Sir Robert, 'the nuclear boys argue the same justification.'

'This was different,' said Paul doggedly. 'I was merely trying to produce an instant antidote to the sort of pestilence we could be faced with in the event of a Third World War. After all, germ warfare is the ideal weapon provided it is virulent enough. A population can be disposed of yet its cities will remain standing and its wealth intact, a far more pleasing prospect to any aggressor than a nuclear wasteland.'

Sir Robert fumbled with another cigarette.

'I have been authorised from on high,' he said, 'to ask you to engineer mutant bacilli to counteract the archaic strain before the whole population has to be consigned to the communal pyres.' He looked at Paul with a sardonic smile. 'Another chance to display your patriotic duty.'

Paul grinned back.

'Baron Frankenstein can't wait to start,' he said. 'But there is the question of facilities. SEMs and EMAs and micro-lasers are pretty rare pieces of equipment.'

'I'll arrange all that. This project has the highest priority. What is now required is that you get your strength back to undertake the programme.'

'The thought of getting back to work makes me feel a new man already,' said Paul.

13

The Prime Minister has protested to the EEC Commission following the announcement by France that any British aircraft entering French airspace will be shot down. This warning follows an attempt by members of a hang-gliding club to cross the Channel. In London, the Chief Medical Officer has denied rumours that Haffkine vaccine is proving ineffective. And now back to Lifeline . . .

Apart from dying of it, the worst aspect of the plague was how quickly one accepted it, Charity decided as, with a medical mask over the lower half of her face, she drove her battered Mercedes along Fleet Street. Once it had held a special magic for her – a magic reflected by the offices of the great daily newspapers, the bars where seemingly blasé journalists discussed the story behind the story, and the choked side streets where trucks unloaded huge rolls of newsprint.

Now the newspaper offices had closed, their reduced editions being printed in the provinces. The jostling crowd which had always seemed as though it were racing against some collective deadline had gone – and the word 'deadline' had become a sick joke. But what alarmed Charity as she manoeuvred round an overturned milk float was the realisation that she had grown accustomed to this desolation.

Passing the black-glassed walls of the *Daily Express*, she saw a pedestrian reel and collapse in the gutter. A few weeks ago she would have braked and run to his aid, but now she drove on in the knowledge that there was nothing she could do. If she felt anything it was resentment against the victim for making her aware of her loss of pity. By the time she reached Aldwych she had seen two corpses lying in doorways.

Perhaps it was exhaustion which had numbed her feelings. She worked harder as the staff on Radio City dwindled. It was believed that Trevor Jones, forewarned by a soaring temperature, had calmly walked to the Embankment and then thrown himself off Waterloo Bridge. Another to have vanished was Tim Holt, the programme controller. After a stint of several days at the station he had gone to his Chelsea flat to renew his wardrobe and enjoy a night's rest. Next morning Vic Kelly received a tearful phone call from the friend who shared his apartment. 'Poor Timothy's gone,' was all the boy could manage to say between his sobs.

'That's a turn-up for the book,' commented Vic. 'I'd never have guessed.'

Somehow the survivors managed to keep the station on the air, and when Charity or Phil felt too exhausted to continue in front of the microphone they put on long symphonies or operas. As the plague became more virulent an increasing number of listeners rang up requesting programmes of classical music. 'Music to die to,' Phil Jason had muttered, regretting the days when he had played little else but the Top Twenty.

Rounding Aldwych, Charity drove up Kingsway to Russell Square where she parked in front of an incongruously modern building guarded by a silver-suited sentry with an automatic rifle.

'Please see that nobody sets my poor car alight,' she said as she passed through the plate glass doors on which discreet gold script read 'University of London Biology Department'.

In the reception area a uniformed commissionaire, masked like herself, nodded as she went to the lift. Although he had always been civil to her, there was something about him which she put down as 'bad vibes'. Since the equality laws had been passed the racially prejudiced were careful to conceal their feelings but no legislation can alter mental attitudes and occasionally Charity felt a psychic shock when secret hostility was directed against her. Today she was too tired to care what the commissionaire thought – the only important thing was that in a few moments she would be with Paul.

Lancelot Storm sat with several fellow commanders at an oval table in the high-ceilinged Belgravia apartment, trying to disguise his exultation at being invited to the Leader's home. Wagnerian music poured from hidden loudspeakers. In one corner of the sumptuous room stood a Bluthner on which were arranged silver-framed portraits, mostly of young men whose confident smiles suggested they really did believe tomorrow belonged to them. Above the marble fireplace was a gilded carving of an eagle, the lightning bolt symbol in its talons indicating it had once graced an SS officers' mess. The paintings by English landscape artists were highly detailed and sentimental, and Lancelot remembered that the Leader regarded modern art as yet another manifestation of how Zion had poisoned the great traditions of the West.

The volume of *Siegfried* was lowered, an oak-panelled door opened and there was the Leader, an old man with world-weary features belied by the intensity of his pale blue eyes.

'Be seated, gentlemen,' he said, fitting a cigarette into a long holder. 'Let me offer you refreshment.'

He reached out his right hand, on which Lancelot noticed he wore a silver ring in the shape of the NBP symbol, and pressed an ivory bellpush mounted on the table. A moment later a young man in a white coat appeared who was not only the Leader's bodyservant but also his bodyguard.

'Max, see what our guests will have to drink, will you, and then bring the large-scale map. Now, gentlemen, I have summoned you here to tell you frankly that we are faced with a crisis. The plague has claimed a third of our membership and, although recruiting has been phenomenal since the outbreak, we cannot go on losing experienced, well-drilled veterans at this rate. So what do you have to say to that?'

For a long minute it seemed that they had nothing to say

and then Lancelot, encouraged by the glow of the Chivas Regal he had just downed, remarked that it was doubtful if anyone could do anything about the plague. The neo-Marxists had probably lost a similar proportion of their membership. The only answer, as he could see it, was for the surviving members to become more dedicated, more ready to accept the challenge when The Day of National Rebirth came. No matter how many fell, the Party must achieve its objective by sheer triumph of the will.

It was a heroic little speech straight from the heart, and Lancelot was encouraged to see that the Leader smiled slightly as he drank his iced Perrier water.

'You are correct, comrade-in-arms,' he said in a voice that was always soft unless he was before a row of microphones. 'Bubonic plague is no respecter of party lines, yet if we could find a way to avoid infection not only would we remain numerically strong but it would impress upon the sickly public that we are a *Corps d'élite*. Therefore, gentlemen, I decree that the Party must become immune, and immune we will march through the present chaos to establish the New Order.'

He paused, looking from face to face with a curious smile.

'You may be asking yourselves how it could be possible. The answer lies in a serum that is being developed at the university biological laboratory. I have the information direct from one of our founder members who during the day works as a commissionaire there, a man whose simple and unquestioning loyalty gives me confidence in what he has reported. In other words, gentlemen, he is too stupid to lie.

'Over the past few days he has been in touch with me regarding the development of this new serum. As it is obvious that the vaccine which has been used so far is ineffective, time has been of the essence in the production of a new strain and this morning our commissionaire told me that the first batch is nearing completion. The moment that it is ready for use we will mount a raid on the laboratory, and through the good offices of Dr Schwarz every member of our organisation will be inoculated.

'I have brought you here today to discuss our strategy in entering the building which, because of the high priority of the project, is guarded. I might add that the interruption of this programme will accelerate the public's loss of faith in its leaders. Without the serum the death toll will continue to mount, people will be demoralised and therefore all the more ready to accept our authority when The Day comes. I would suggest, therefore, that before you leave the laboratory you ensure the unique equipment necessary for this work is permanently out of action. Nor do your troopers need to be restrained in their treatment of the scientific team, several members of which have the taint of Zion while the man who heads the project makes no secret of the fact that he has a black mistress.

'Commander Storm, when you get the signal I want your Eagle Commando to parade in Russell Square. Meanwhile other comrades-in-arms will assemble nearby in mufti . . . '

As the Leader continued to outline his plan Lancelot gave a mental prayer of thanks to his Aryan gods. At last the time for action was at hand.

'I do apologise for my hair,' said Charity as she and Paul sat over cups of tea in the laboratory's canteen. 'It badly needs straightening but when I went to my hairdresser this morning the place was burnt out.'

'You don't need to apologise,' said Paul. 'I always thought an Afro style would suit you better. Anyway, you're not the only one whose appearance has changed.'

He ran his fingers over the short beard which he had allowed to grow since his illness. Charity tried to hide the expression of anxiety on her face as she looked at him. If the plague had hollowed his cheeks and made him lose weight, the tension and lack of sleep resulting from his round-the-clock laboratory work had etched lines upon his face. And if his face had been white after the illness, fatigue had made it an unhealthy grey. She noticed with alarm that when he lifted his cup his hands were shaking.

'How is progress today?' she asked, keeping her voice bright and confident.

'We're nearly there. I've got a mutant strain which when introduced to rats – the classical vectors of plague – gives them immunity to the type of bacilli which came from the plague pit.' He rubbed the back of his hand wearily across his eyes. 'In ordinary circumstances there should be exhaustive tests running over a period of months before one would try it on a human being. But we don't have the time, and I don't mind admitting the prospect terrifies me in case there are consequences outside our calculations.'

'Darling,' she said, taking his hand, 'the military say that the death roll has reached over a million now. No matter what the side effects may be, the plague is the real enemy and to overcome it is worth any risk.'

He nodded soberly.

'You're right, of course, but it goes against all my training and professional experience.' He glanced at his watch. 'Time to check the cultures. Do you want to see what I have been brewing up?'

Charity followed him into the large room filled with equipment whose functions she could not understand. As he talked of using a special laser to alter the gene pattern within micro-organisms, of DNA manipulation and transplantation of molecules to alter the structure of *Pasteurella pestis* cells, she felt as she did when a child trying to imagine the universe being endless. It was outside her comprehension. On another level it was disturbing that the rather simple easy-going man she had fallen in love with was in fact a scientific genius. What she subconsciously resented was that part of his mind was at home in a world which to her seemed more fantastic than anything she had come across in science fiction novels.

'These are my babies,' he said, taking her to a closed circuit television monitor connected to an electron microscope. He adjusted the controls and on the screen she saw a confusion of spindle-like shapes within translucent blobs of agar gel in which the culture was growing.

'Now you've developed the anti-plague bacteria, how are you going to produce enough to immunise millions of people?'

'By using the resources of a commercial company called

Bio-Synthetics.'

'Are those the people who are producing protein and lubricants by farming bacteria?'

He laughed.

'That's the way the Press would probably describe it. It's one of the answers to the fossilised fuel crisis. Mac has already gone to their place at Gayton in Northamptonshire to prepare the vats for mass production of AP-13 – as we call the mutant strain. Under the right conditions the bacilli reproduce at an astronomical rate, and we estimate that within ten days of the basic strain arriving there the immunisation programme can be started. If all goes well I'll take it to Bio-Synthetics tomorrow or the day after.' He pointed to the far end of the long room where, behind a plate glass partition, masked and gowned laboratory assistants were harvesting bacteria culture from petri dishes into a special solution which was then decanted into insulated containers.

A young man came over to them and said, 'Excuse me, Dr Mitchell, but I thought you'd better see the latest print-out on the enzyme factor.'

'Thanks, Simon,' said Paul and wearily took the concertina-folded paper.

'I must be getting back to the station,' said Charity.

Paul nodded absently, his forefinger running along the lines of computer symbols.

'Before I go there's just one thing I want to say,' she continued.

'Of course, darling.'

'When you're ready to go to Gayton I'm going to drive you there. I hope your part will be over then, and I'm going to make sure that you recuperate. Also it comes within my line of duty. I'm putting together a feature on AP-13.'

'I think it's a splendid idea for us to have some time together in the country. Before you leave we'll see Simon Bernstein; he knows the drill about getting medical passes.'

'All right, darling,' she said and kissed him. At that moment the lab was invaded.

'Oh dear oh Lord, will you look at that lot!' chuckled the

soldier on guard at the doorway of the Biology Department laboratory to the commissionaire standing beside him. 'NBP troopers – I'd just love to see how that lot would make out in a bit of real action, like in Ulster.'

Across the Russell Square gardens marched the Eagle Commando behind the Union Jack, and beside the standard bearer strode Lancelot Storm, his stern face masking a turmoil of hopes and fears. If in reality things worked with the precision of the planning, there was a chance he would be in line for a Sword of Valour after The Day had dawned and the NPB was in control. He could imagine walking up to a podium in the Albert Hall while thousands sang the new version of 'Land of Hope and Glory'. But this was not time for daydreams, no matter how heroic. At his crisp order the commando halted on the north side of the square, facing the laboratory building.

The sentry watched with amusement while the super-troopers spaced out and snapped to attention. For a moment his gaze wandered as he caught sight of a convoy of army trucks heading down Southampton Row in what had come to be known callously as 'The Stiff Patrol'. Then a small group of women turned into Russell Square from Bedford Way and approached the steps he was guarding.

'Is this the office?' demanded one of them.

'Office, Miss?' said the soldier.

'You know, the office,' the woman repeated. She came up the steps holding out a piece of paper, followed by her companions.

'You'd better let me see that,' said the commissionaire.

She held out the paper with some casual remark, and four women hurled themselves upon the startled guard.

'Here,' he protested as he felt himself walled in by female bodies, their arms round his neck in an attempt to drag him down.

'Lend a hand, Jim,' he shouted to the commissionaire, but the commissionaire's response was to seize his automatic rifle. He stood back while the reeling group of women swept the soldier through the doorway.

Immediately Lancelot Storm shouted, 'Eagle Commando for-ward!' At the double the super-troopers crossed the road and swarmed into the foyer. Several detached themselves to take charge of the sentry now sprawled on his back. The commissionaire returned to the steps where he casually surveyed the square as though nothing had happened.

'Guard squad remain here, special detail follow me,' Lancelot ordered and then paused. Where the hell was Dr Schwarz? His panic died when he saw an old man in a shabby raincoat being ushered in by the commissionaire. 'Hurry, doctor,' he cried and led his special group of ten down the corridor towards the bacteriological laboratory. In his mind he could see the plan of the building which had been provided by the helpful commissionaire.

'Arms,' he said briefly and they produced pistols from their pockets. Originally these had been replica Lugers but the NPB armourer had converted them by inserting lengths of barrel sawn from .22 sporting rifles. Unfortunately it meant that they were single-shot weapons, but those about to be held up were unlikely to realise this.

'Barnet! Mackenzie! In you go!'

Immediately the two biggest men hurled themselves through the double doors and shouted to the astonished laboratory workers to freeze. NBP tacticians had studied the methods of professional terrorists and were aware of the advantage of surprise and shock. As Lancelot Storm marched through the doorway several of his men pushed over racks containing glass retorts so the crash of breaking equipment heightened the effect.

The intruders fanned out and took up strategic positions, each having singled out an individual to aim at. Everything happened so fast and so unexpectedly that the staff stood paralysed by their benches. Only Paul Mitchell strode forward angrily.

'Stand where you are,' ordered Lancelot, 'or I shall have no hesitation in shooting you. Our mission is of such importance that in comparison your life is immaterial.'

Adrenalin surging through Paul's system would have carried him on had not Charity seized him by the arm.

'Cool it, Paul,' she hissed, and they remained frozen halfway between the technicians and the super-troopers.

Lancelot looked with scorn at the black girl, then his eyes flicked over the rest of their prisoners, several of whom, he noted, were of degenerate Semitic blood.

'By the authority of the National Emergency Council I am here to requisition the supply of the anti-plague vaccine code-named AP-13 which I know you have manufactured here. Hand over your stock to Dr Schwarz and you will not be harmed.'

'What national council?' demanded Paul, his anger finding expression in his voice. 'And who the hell are you ersatz SS freaks to break into my laboratory?'

'Rolf!'

The youth who had formerly borne the standard stepped forward smartly and swung his arm so his pistol foresight sliced Paul's cheek. He stepped back just as smartly.

As though unable to believe what was happening, Paul put his fingertips to the wound. He felt he was a participant in a nightmare which was half a century out of date.

'You see I mean business,' declared Lancelot, allowing his gaze to travel severely round the shocked faces of the others. He expected that several would soon be grovelling. 'Let that be a lesson, Dr Mitchell. We are utterly sincere in our intentions and ready to demonstrate our axiom that victory is the natural inheritance of the strong.'

Paul was about to make a retort but controlled himself as Charity's fingers dug into his arm.

'There is no point in prolonging this,' continued Lancelot, his confidence mushrooming with the dizzy elation of having people in his power for the first time in his life. 'Deliver up your supply of AP-13 immediately, otherwise I shall take appropriate steps to locate it.'

Simon Bernstein stepped from behind his bench.

'Wherever you got your information from,' he said mildly, 'it was incorrect. As yet we have not succeeded in producing a culture which will provide immunisation against archaic *Pasteurella pestis*.'

Lancelot permitted himself a steely smile.

'Do you think I would believe a Jew?' he demanded. 'My information is impeccable.' He nodded to two of his men who stepped forward and, using the karate learned during

Tuesday evening combat sessions, sent Simon crashing to the floor with a moan of pure agony.

'Now attend to that trash,' Lancelot ordered. 'I think Dr Mitchell may change his mind in the next few minutes.'

The two super-troopers seized Charity by the arms and dragged her to a bench on which a bunsen burner hissed gently. One held her tightly while the other picked up the burner, adjusting it so that its blue flame glowed like that of a welding torch.

'Dr Mitchell, you can save your whore pain and disfigurement by handing over the AP-13.'

'Bastard!' shouted Paul and, without Charity to restrain him, flung himself at the NBP commander with a desperate notion of seizing his gun. He had only gone two steps when a karate chop on the back of his neck felled him. Charity screamed and struggled out of the clutch of the super-trooper.

'Paul,' she cried wildly, then turning on Lancelot she shouted, 'You murderer – you've killed him!'

From his position on the laboratory floor Paul struggled to form words of warning but it seemed the scientifically applied blow had paralysed him. He could only watch with horror as Rolf, the standard-bearer, clubbed her down with the reinforced butt of his pistol. Without a sound Charity collapsed to the floor a few feet from where Paul lay.

The violence of the last few seconds had a strange effect on Lancelot. His pulses hammered an atavistic hymn of hatred within his head. Lying before him was the embodiment of all that he – and the elect before him – sought to cleanse from the world, the *untermensch* which prevented the great Aryan race from fulfilling its destiny. Some of the tension coiled within him communicated itself to the others. The only sound in the laboratory came from the bunsen burner as the leader of the eagle Commando raised his once-toy Luger and sighted it at Charity's head.

'Stop,' screamed Simon Bernstein from a kneeling position. 'I'll give you the AP-13.'

With a sigh Lancelot Storm lowered his pistol. As was to be expected the Jew had begun to grovel. He nodded and a super-trooper helped him to his feet. Weaving like a drunken man, he crossed to the laboratory freezer and flung open the door. 'There,' he said, pointing to a cylindrical container on which the letters AP and some code numbers had been scrawled with a red chinagraph pencil.

'Dr Schwarz,' said Lancelot.

The man in the raincoat walked forward, unscrewed the insulated container and drew out a hermetically-sealed jar containing a creamy fluid. He nodded, screwed the cap back into position and picked up the container by its carrying handle. Without a word he left the laboratory.

'Back up against the wall,' Lancelot ordered the chalk-faced staff. 'Phase two!' he added and stepped back. Ignoring the two huddled forms on the floor, the troopers systematically destroyed the laboratory. Racks of equipment crashed to the floor. Microscopic apparatus which had cost hundreds of thousands of pounds was battered to junk. Short-handled hatchets, specially brought in under tunics for the purpose, were wielded against the unique laser machine until it disintegrated in a firework display of sparks. In one corner a flask of petrol turned the laboratory's records into a bonfire.

Watching from the doorway, Lancelot Storm experienced an orgiastic sense of elation he had never been able to achieve with the opposite sex. It was as though he were a shining blade of pure destruction cutting out the cancer of the world. He had joined the ranks of heroes who until this moment had existed only in old black-and-white newsreels. As smoke began to billow through the laboratory he managed to return to reality. His task was complete, the AP-13 had been collected and the equipment capable of making further supplies destroyed.

'Phase Three!'

He led his men down the corridor and out of the building to where a number of vehicles waited to spirit them away to secret destinations. Glancing at his watch as the laundry van in which he lay sped north up Tottenham Court Road, Lancelot was amazed to find the whole operation had taken place in less than ten minutes.

Charity opened her eyes to see a circle of black faces gazing down at her, some framed by dread-locks flowing from beneath knitted caps. For a moment she had no idea where she was. Superimposed in her mind was a picture of Paul lying on the laboratory floor beneath the gloating gaze of the tubby man in the home-made uniform.

'You all right, sister?' came a voice from above. She turned her head and saw they were in an untidy courtyard at the back of an abandoned pub. Somebody had rolled up a jacket as a pillow for her.

'I think I am,' she said as strong hands reached down to help her into a sitting position. 'What am I doing here?'

A man in a black jacket with 'Daddy Kool' emblazoned upon it said, 'We saved you from that honky bastard, sister. He must have done you no good.'

She shook her head to try and clear it.

'What happened, boys?'

'We was just cruising an' we see this honk carrying you,' replied Daddy Kool. 'He must have given you one bad time 'cos you were out for the count. But we took care of him.'

The others sniggered at the memory.

'When we finished you wasn't the only one out for the count,' another interjected. 'We brought you here to wake up where the fuzz ain't likely to interfere.'

'Oh, my God,' said Charity. 'Where did you leave the man who was carrying me?'

'Did he rape you, sister?' someone demanded.

'Where did you leave him?' she repeated.

'We didn't leave him no place,' said Daddy Kool to a background of laughter. 'After we put him bye-byes we hid the evidence, sister. It's untidy to leave bodies around in the streets. Spoils the look of this great white city. So we sacked him up and threw him into a dead cart. He'll be fryin' tonight.'

14

'Happiness . . . is luxury hotels with fabulous pools and fantastic golf courses. Happiness . . . is watching the sunset from a beach of white sand. Happiness . . . is good food, good drinks – and your own special friend. Fly to heaven with Air Bermuda.'

Bloody hell!

Sorry, wrong tape. Must be losing my grip . . .

In the Belgravia apartment Max uncorked champagne and the Leader toasted Lancelot Storm and the men who had taken over the laboratory.

'By your action, you have ensured the invulnerability of our movement,' he declared. 'While others die around us we shall be free to carry on our work in the building of a new society out of the ruins of the old one. When that day comes your heroism will not be forgotten.'

Again the music of 'Land of Hope and Glory' (revised) swelled within Lancelot's head.

'At this very moment,' continued the Leader, 'Dr Schwarz is inoculating the rank and file.' He fingered his upper arm tenderly. 'It is relatively painless. Your turn will come when the doctor returns from the barracks.

'Now this strike is successfully completed we must prepare for the next step towards gaining control of the city. It is essential that we are able to communicate our aims and demands to the demoralised population and therefore, comrades-in-arms, the next target will be Radio City.'

Reluctantly Paul floated back to consciousness on a black tide of pain. He had no idea where he was and very little of who he was. All he wanted was to return to blessed oblivion, to feel nothing, to remember nothing and to do nothing. But his pain-racked body rebelled against his mind and gradually physical awareness forced reality upon him. Apart from the pain in his neck where he had been struck by the super-trooper, the whole of his body ached with blows he had received from the gang which had materialised when he had carried the unconscious Charity from the burning laboratory.

He tried to ascertain the extent of his injuries, terrified by the fact that when he opened his eyes he remained in total darkness. Had the blows to his head blinded him? His immediate reaction was to lift his hands to his face but for some reason he could not move. Was he paralysed as well? And what comprised the mixture of soft angular substances he felt enveloping him? And why was the silence so intense he could hear the beat of his heart?

For a long time he lay, endeavouring to go step by step through memory but betrayed by his lack of concentration. His shallow breathing became faster and faster, sweat soaked his clothing as a result of mysterious heat generated about him and his mind drifted into a dreamland. He was on a white boat sailing on a perfectly straight stream through an enchanted landscape, a landscape without colour but etched in black and white like a drawing by Aubrey Beardsley. He turned his head to the profile of the woman seated beside him, a profile like the mask of an Egyptian princess and as black as the water on which the white boat sailed.

When his eyes opened again to the darkness he was in a higher state of consciousness. He could no longer lie there passively – he had to know what had happened to him or all would be lost. With sudden inspiration he put out his tongue and found himself licking plastic. A thrill of terror swamped his mind for a moment. Suddenly things were falling into place. Pictures flashed through his mind with the rapidity of cards flipping over in a Victorian peepshow, crystallising the terrible knowledge of what had happened.

A sob tore from his throat with the realisation that, trapped in a body bag, he lay among plague victims awaiting cremation.

In the exhaustion which followed the panic, in which he struggled to free himself from the enveloping plastic, he managed to think clearly. It was futile to spend his remaining strength squirming like a gaffed fish, his only hope lay in drawing attention to himself. At all costs he must stay awake so that when the time came for him to be moved he could shout for help . . . unless he and the corpses about him were already in position to be sprayed with petrol. In a new paroxysm of terror he sniffed, but in the confines of the bag there was only the reek of his own sweat and fear.

Sometimes his heart accelerated in expectation when he felt movement close to him, until he realised it was only the post-mortem convulsion of a corpse.

As time passed he became calmer. Now the stupidity of the situation obsessed him. The work which should have brought hope to millions had been undone in a few moments, and because a group of blacks had mistaken his intentions he was to be cheated out of perhaps forty years of life.

Inexorably his mind went over and over the details of the raid, the way Charity had crumpled beside him as he lay paralysed on the floor, and the near hysterical voice of Simon Bernstein as he led the raiders to the vaccine store. Was his act of betrayal because generations of persecution had eaten into his genes so that, when faced with the type of men who revelled in pogroms, his will collapsed? Paul could hardly believe it. Simon had come from Tel Aviv and an Israeli was unlikely to be intimidated by racist bullies. Yet the fact remained that through his action NPB members would be the only ones in Britain immune from plague.

Despite his endeavours to stay awake, Paul began to doze. When a shifting of the shapes imprisoning him caused his eyes to open to the inevitable blackness he was not sure whether he had been unconscious for a few seconds or an hour. Before he could cry for help the weight of a corpse above him was removed, followed by tearing sounds as a blade slit the imprisoning plastic. But what happened in the next minute remained a nightmare for the rest of his life.

As the knife hissed past his face Paul was aware of a strip of luminosity caused by distant arc lights. A pair of hands pulled the plastic flaps apart and he was looking up at his deliverer. It was a strange figure dressed entirely in black, its face hooded like a member of the SAS on night manoeuvres. For a moment the eyes in the mask-holes gazed down at Paul, but when he tried to mutter his gratitude the man answered with an oath of surprise. Instead of trying to raise Paul from the shrouded forms surrounding him, he knelt on his chest and, seizing his hair in his left hand, jerked his head to one side to enable him to cut his throat with the Stanley knife in his right hand.

Somewhere a rifle cracked. Blood rained on to Paul's face as the figure jerked away like a marionette whose strings had been snatched by a child. Moments later a voice shouted through the night, 'I've killed the filthy bastard!' Other voices mingled incomprehensibly and then someone said, 'Let's see what he was up to.' And this time Paul found himself looking up at a soldier in a silver anti-contamination suit.

'Thank God, we've found him,' the man cried through his mask. 'He's alive all right. Come and help me, Harry.'

Paul found himself half carried, half dragged down the quaking mound of bodies. Batteries of floodlights, which told him that he was at the Wembley Stadium, illuminated the bizarre scene as army bulldozers shovelled corpses towards the cremation pits. In the distance a Rolls Royce was incongruously parked by a line of petrol tankers.

The next thing he knew he was in what had once been a dressing room and an army sergeant was offering him a glass of brandy.

'That man who found me,' gasped Paul. 'Why did he . . . ?'

'A pervert, sir,' said the sergeant. 'We've had several of these necros sneak in. They black-up and creep about in the shadows, opening body bags in the hope of finding young women. At least we can be grateful he found you. There's been a young black lady here – the one with the radio programme – and her boss. They said there was a chance somebody had been delivered alive and they've been waiting in the hope that we'd find you. It was like looking for a needle in a haystack.'

Vic Kelly walked through the door. 'Stone the crows, sport, you look like something from beyond the Black Stump,' he exclaimed. 'Charity's waiting for you in the car. These army blokes won't let her near you until you've been disinfected, but they knew I wasn't likely to kiss you . . . not after where you'd been!'

'Wake up, Paul, wake up,' cried Charity, refraining in the nick of time from shaking his bruised shoulder. At her excited voice he opened his eyes painfully and smiled with relief at finding himself in her flat after the previous night's ordeal.

'Paul, it's terribly important,' she continued. 'Simon Bernstein has been on the telephone. Apparently he's been going crazy trying to locate you. He wants you to get over to the laboratory as fast as you can.'

'What laboratory?' said Paul. 'And what can he be excited about since he gave our SS pals the AP-13?'

'I think he did that to save our lives.'

'I can't see the point. The serum's stolen, the only equipment capable of engineering bacteria in the country is smashed beyond repair, our notes are destroyed and the laboratory razed. I think I'd just rather remain with you for the duration.'

'All right, but I'm going to see what it's all about. My voices tell me that today is going to be very important. Oh, and he said for us to get our health passes.'

'Coffee first then,' Paul grumbled as he painfully eased himself up in bed. 'If I look anything like I feel it can't be a pretty sight.'

Within an hour he was beside Charity in the Mercedes heading in the direction of Russell Square.

'If we meet any more of your rasta friends please tell them I'm not hostile,' Paul said. 'Hell! Look at that pack of dogs. On second thoughts, don't!'

About twenty animals, once household pets but turned feral by starvation, were barking and fighting round something in the doorway of a boarded-up shop. Paul looked back to make sure there was no life left in the body they were savaging while Charity pressed her foot hard on the accelerator.

'It's those pariahs which keep the streets deserted,' she said. 'They are worse than wolves once they get the taste of human meat.'

To take her mind off the sight they had just witnessed Paul pressed a pre-set button on the radio and the failing voice of Phil Jason filled the car.

'The building looks intact,' said Charity as they turned into Russell Square. 'The way the lab was burning I should have thought it would have been razed to the ground.'

They left the car and walked into the unguarded foyer where Simon Bernstein was reclining in one of the luxurious reception chairs.

'Hi,' he greeted. 'Nice to see you're both alive.'

'What is this, Simon?' asked Paul shortly. 'Have you been to the lab?'

'Sure. Come and look for yourself.'

They followed him down the corridor and into the laboratory – the place was full of the sour smell that lingers when a fire has been extinguished with water.

'It seems a sprinkler system came on after our panic exit,' he said.

'So?' said Paul with a shrug. 'What difference does it make? We can't develop any more vaccines here.'

'There's no need to,' Simon said. 'The AP-13 serum is still intact, though I'm rather worried about the variations in its temperature.'

'What do you mean? I heard you handing it over to the NBP.'

Simon chuckled as though he'd just remembered a joke.

'I shouldn't laugh, and perhaps I may live to ask God for forgiveness,' he said. 'But the cylinder they took contained our supply of live *Pasteurella pestis* bacilli.'

'You mean . . . ?' gasped Paul, his voice expressing his sudden understanding.

'That's right. By now their tame doctor will have inoculated them with untreated plague germs. The old fool was too excited or too stupid to check our record numbers against those on the container. Perhaps he thought I really was too terrified to think of lying to them – an error of which our neo-Nazi friends will soon be aware.'

'And the AP-13?'

'Intact,' said Simon. He opened the blackened door of a refrigerator and pointed to a canister. 'All ready for you to take to Sir Robert at Bio-Synthetics.'

'That was brilliant.'

Simon shrugged.

'I owed them,' he said.

Charity slowed the car when the red and white pole of the army checkpoint came into sight. Situated at the intersection of London Road and the A5, it was a picture of military neatness. A large sign above the prefabricated office read REPORT HERE FOR MEDICAL CLEARANCE. The two soldiers who had removed their decontamination helmets for a smoke looked bored, the only hint of menace being a Saracen armoured car parked discreetly in the background.

'Your business, sir?' asked a lieutenant politely as they placed their passes on the counter.

'I'm taking medical samples to Gayton,' Paul explained.

'I don't know how important it is but I'd advise you not to try. Beyond this frontier post it's a state of bloody anarchy. The local people have got up vigilante patrols to mop up the refugees that get past us. I've only a few men and one vehicle, so it's impossible to offer you an escort.'

'We'll just have to risk it,' said Charity. 'I'm sure when we explain our mission we'll have no trouble.'

The officer looked up at her from under bushy eyebrows.

'I hope you'll find it so, miss,' he said. 'But yesterday they shot up one of *our* convoys so I do advise you not to go any further. Beyond that barber's pole it's a no-go area and, crazy as it sounds, you'd be safer back in London.'

Charity shrugged.

'They're stopping the white trains coming out now,' he added in a final attempt to dissuade them. 'Some maniacs have even ripped up the lines.'

He shrugged and called through the window, 'Okay, boys,

let 'em through.'

On the road north past Elstree abandoned cars became more and more frequent. Signs had been crudely daubed on their panels reading TURN BACK! NO LONDONERS PAST THIS POINT! YOU HAVE BEEN WARNED!

With her bottom lip between her teeth Charity drove while Paul sat tense with the laboratory container between his knees. She began to slow when ahead of them she saw a line of overturned cars obstructing most of the highway. Above the narrow gap in the middle a banner, obviously the work of a professional signpainter, read HALT – THIS IS A PLAGUE-FREE AREA – NO ENTRY.

Standing in the gap were two middle-aged men armed with shotguns. Charity pulled up with the nose of the Mercedes in front of the entrance. While one man kept them covered, the other came forward scowling. Both had handkerchiefs over the lower halves of their faces.

'Can't you sods read?' he demanded. 'The signs down the road told you to turn back.'

A third man appeared, a notebook in his hand. 'It's a London registration all right.'

'Go back where you came from,' said the first man. 'And don't have any notions about stopping on the side of the road and going cross country. Our patrols have dogs and they'll soon flush you out.'

'I think there's some misunderstanding,' said Paul, trying to keep his voice even. 'Here are our certificates of health.'

'How much did you pay for them on the Black Market?'

'Look, I can sympathise with your wish to keep your area free but this is a special case. I'm a doctor and I have to take this serum to Gayton. It's in your own interest I go through.'

'Is that the best you can do?' demanded the scowling man. 'We hear stories better than that every day, don't we, boys?' The men nodded. 'And if you're really a doctor it means you're more likely to be carrying the infection than most.'

'Please,' said Charity, 'you've got to believe us.'

'I don't have to believe you. All I have to believe is what

our anti-plague committee says and the anti-plague committee says that no one – but no one – can enter this zone. Now, if you don't sod off I'll put both barrels through your windscreen, and it won't be the first time I've done it.'

Again his companions nodded in grave agreement.

'All right,' said Charity with a sigh. She put the car into reverse and slowly backed away, stopped and slipped it into forward gear.

'Duck,' she hissed. Next instant her foot was hard down on the accelerator and the car leapt forwards. Taken by surprise, the men scattered as the Mercedes hurtled through the gap, scoring its side panels against one of the overturned cars.

'Keep down, darling,' Charity shouted as shotgun pellets rattled against the boot. 'We'll soon be out of range.'

As they dwindled from sight one of the men began speaking urgently into a walkie-talkie.

'No turning back now,' laughed Paul, sitting upright. 'I must say, darling, you were magnificent. With luck we should be at Gayton in half an hour at this rate.'

'Provided there's no more barricades,' Charity said. 'Oh-oh, it looks as though we've got followers,' she added as she looked in the rear vision mirror.

Paul turned and saw that two motor cyclists, alerted by the barrier guards, had emerged from a side road and were racing head-down in pursuit.

'Let me try a trick,' said Charity. 'It always works in the movies.'

She eased her foot off the accelerator to enable the motor cyclists to get within a few feet of them, then snapped on the sidelights. Seeing two rear lights suddenly glow red, the motor cyclists braked while Charity accelerated away at full power. One of the riders skidded off the road but the other continued, the noise of his powerful Honda reaching them above the roar of the wind.

Rounding a curve, Charity gave an exclamation of dismay as she saw another road-block ahead of them.

'Trapped,' she muttered and this time she stamped on her brake pedal for real. The heavy car screeched to a stop and the motor cyclist, not believing the stop lights until it was too late, swerved wildly to avoid them. The rear wing tipped his machine as he screeched past, and he was catapulted over the handlebars as his front wheel struck the kerb. Charity wrenched the steering wheel and made a tight U-turn.

'There's nothing for it but to go back, Paul,' she said. He nodded grimly.

'It's not just us, darling,' he said, 'but . . . ' He tapped the container.

'Let's hope those self-appointed guards down there haven't thought of blocking the gap,' said Charity as the speedometer needle swung towards the 80 -miles-an-hour mark.

Within a couple of minutes the barricade was in sight. Alerted by the throaty sound of the Mercedes' engine, the guards raised their shotguns. One stood in the centre of the gap aiming his barrels straight at the windscreen.

Charity slowed the car to aim at the narrow entrance and was hardly aware of the hail of shot striking the bonnet. What alarmed her was the shotgun aimed straight at the windscreen.

When he realised thcy did not intend to stop the man had fired both barrels, but his fear of the two tons of steel hurtling towards him spoiled his aim. The main flight of pellets passed over the car but several struck the windscreen with enough velocity to transform the shatterproof glass into a thousand crystals. With the view ahead suddenly blotted out, Charity held the wheel firmly. Miraculously the car stayed on course and passed through the gap with inches to spare on either side. A soft thud told them that the man who had guarded the gap had not been able to scramble out of the way in time. The impact hurled him into the air like a broken doll thrown up by a child.

Simultaneously Charity and Paul punched their fists through the opaque screen in the approved manner. Cascades of safety-glass fragments were blown inwards, but Charity had a view of the road again, and by jerking the wheel was able to prevent them careering into a fence. Tongues of blood creeping towards them over the white bonnet made her wince but she did not lower her speed until the army checkpoint came in sight.

'Well, that's it,' said Raymond Carson, walking into The Digger's office. He held a piece of paper torn from the tele-printer. 'The army say they've now incinerated two million bodies in the London area, but they refuse to estimate how many people are lying dead in their homes and haven't been found yet.'

'And how the hell do I announce that?' demanded Phil Jason, following the news editor. 'Hi folks, this is swinging Radio City bringing you all the latest and greatest. And just before we pass on to the Top Ten here's a little item of local interest – since Christmas a sixth of the population has moved on to the great pop festival in the sky by courtesy of Bubonic and the Plague Pits.'

'Phil, sport,' said Vic anxiously, 'I think you need a shot of snake cure.' He crossed to the refrigerator. 'I guess we could all use one come to that. It means, proportionally speaking, that London has already caught up with the 1665 plague totals.'

'But what the hell am I going to play after *Newsflash*?' said Phil moodily as The Digger handed him a glass of brandy.

' "Rock of Ages"?' suggested Raymond. 'I gather religion has increased in popularity over the last few weeks.'

'How about John Lennon's "Imagine"?' said Charity from the doorway.

'Absolutely right,' said Phil. 'I must be slipping not to have thought of it!'

Vic knew why he had not thought of it. His mind had been occupied by the fact that for the last two days he had been ringing his parents' home outside London without getting a reply.

'What are you doing here, girl?' asked Vic. 'I thought you were doing a story on your resurrected professor's wonder cure.'

'He never made it,' she said simply. 'Outside the perimeter it's like the Wars of the Roses.'

The news editor nodded.

'That's right,' he said. 'Villages, towns, counties . . . they're taking the law into their own hands and going UDI. They've lost faith in that shower up in Edinburgh, and it's only through the armed services there's any organisation left at all. At least they're keeping the food supplies moving, and when they break down God help us all.'

Phil Jason looked up at the clock, a replica of which was on every wall in Radio City.

'Time for me to go and make my announcement,' he said and left the room.

'So you weren't able to get the AP-13 to Bio-Synthetics,' mused The Digger. 'What does Paul intend to do about it now?'

'It's impossible to get official help,' said Charity. 'The phones are out of order and if you do get a ringing tone nobody answers. We wanted to get the use of a helicopter from the RAF but somebody's left the phone off the hook. We did get in touch with the army headquarters. They'd be only too happy to escort us there with a couple of tanks if necessary, provided we can get authorisation from the Ministry of Defence.' She shrugged hopelessly and mimicked a tape-recorded voice. ' "The lines to Edinburgh are all engaged. Please ring later."

'Vic, we haven't got time to wait. I don't understand the technicalities but Paul says that if we don't get the AP-13 bacilli to the Bio-Synthetics labs by the day after tomorrow it'll be too late to start the reproductive process. It's something to do with temperatures, I believe.'

'I suppose we could broadcast some sort of appeal for help,' said The Digger doubtfully, 'but since the plague is breaking out all over the British Isles I rather doubt . . . '

Paul doesn't need appeals for help,' said Charity. 'He's worked out a fantastic idea for getting to Gayton but he does need your personal assistance.'

For five minutes The Digger listened impassively while she enthusiastically outlined the plan.

'It sounds to me the sort of idea that would only grab a kamikaze pilot, but I'll give you a hand,' he said. 'The Lord have mercy on your souls if my paintwork gets scratched.'

15

'Leader Rouge à Base: Contact visuel établi – je répète, contact visuel établi, appareil envahisseur modèle Jetstream, immatriculation anglaise, distance approximative 2000 mètres – à vous.'

The Dassault-Breguet Mirage intercepted the executive jet, which had taken off illegally from Stansted Airport, as it crossed the French coastline south of Bologne. The Jetstream's pilot switched off the threats which were crackling in his earphones and gave a V-sign to the fighter.

'Base à Leader Rouge: Annoncez-vous et procédez aux sommations d'usage.'

'Don't worry, he's putting on an act to scare us,' the pilot reassured his passengers who had each paid a fortune to get clear of England.

'That plane is coming very close,' said a girl nervously.

'He'll get tired of it. Once we've called their bluff they'll let us through their airspace.'

'Leader Rouge à Base: Sommations sans effet, l'appareil ne répond pas.'

'Base a Leader Rouge: Armez vos missiles et alignez vous sur sa trajectoire, la Base va lui donner une dernière fois l'ordre d'évacuer notre espace aerien après quoi ce sera à vous de passer à l'action.'

The Mirage dropped behind the Jetstream. The pilot laughed. 'Told you so. They wouldn't have dared . . . '

'Mais mon commandant, c'est un appareil civil, comment puis-je . . . ?'

'Pierre, cette décision n'est pas de votre compétence – cet appareil pourrait mettre la France entière en péril, je vous donne cet ordre en tant qu'officier supérieur – à mon commandement, feu à volonté.'

In the cabin of the Mirage Red Leader pressed a button and a Sidewinder air-to-air missile streaked from beneath its wing.

'Leader Rouge à Base: Missile I activé, impact positif, cible anéantie – je répète, impact positif, cible anéantie . . . over.'

The Mirage banked away from the blazing fragments.

Darkness was thinning in the east as Vic Kelly drove along Hilliard Avenue until he reached a large brick warehouse where he parked. His headlights reflected on the silver body of a Blanik sailplane standing on the forecourt with three dark figures moving about it. He sat in the car mopping his face with a handkerchief until he saw Charity approaching. Making an effort to assume his professional *bonhomie* he leaned over, opened the passenger door and was aware of the distant baying of a pariah pack.

'It's ready to fly,' the girl said triumphantly. 'Paul and Simon Bernstein worked on it through the night. Apparently all they had to do was uncrate it, bolt on the wings and connect up the control cables. Everything seems to work, and Paul is ready to take off as soon as it's light enough.'

'Rather you than me,' said Vic. 'You make it sound too simple. What's the story if it doesn't get airborne by the time we hit the traffic lights at the end of the avenue?'

'In that case you'll have a glider right up your exhaust pipe. Don't worry, Paul is very confident and he says this westerly breeze will help in getting him aloft. Then we'll be fine if we can make it as far as Wembley.'

'And you'll be up the creek without the proverbial paddle if you don't. There's not that many places you can make a landing in the heart of London. Can't understand why that joker is putting you to such a risk.'

'Because I'm forcing him to take me,' Charity said, tapping the Uher tape recorder. 'I'm following this story to the bitter end and I told him that you would only agree to help if I went with him.'

'You're going to do a live commentary?' he asked as he noticed a throat microphone in her hand.

'This is for my exclusive on How the Plague was Beaten,' she said.

'May we live to hear it,' The Digger said softly. 'So your enthusiasm for radio has returned. No more plans for TV.'

'I've had enough of television for quite a while, thanks. Besides, now that I'm on the board of Radio City . . . '

'By now you and I probably *are* the board of Radio City,' said Vic. 'Look, your bloke's making signals. Must be ready for off.'

They climbed out of the car and approached the Blanik. Again Charity found the same pleasure in its aerodynamic lines as when she had seen it eased out of a crate and its graceful wings locked into position with titanium bolts. At the prospect of flying his new sailplane, even under such bizarre circumstances, Paul seemed to have shrugged off his load of weariness.

'Roll her into the avenue and let's pray no traffic comes,' he said.

With Charity steadying one wing tip and Simon Bernstein the other, the Blanik was pushed forward on its single landing-wheel into the broad roadway.

'If you back up your car we'll get the towline attached,' said Paul, eyeing the rapidly lightening sky. While Vic attached the end of the nylon rope to the Rolls, Paul explained the rate of acceleration and how, once the Blanik reached its optimum towing speed, he would release the line.

'Good luck, cobber,' said Vic. 'Make it a good story, Charity.' He hauled himself behind the wheel and waited with the engine idling silently.

'Right, darling, in you get.' Paul opened the perspex canopy and she climbed into the front seat where he fastened her safety harness. When her tape recorder was stowed to her satisfaction, he handed her the canister containing the AP-13.

'Right, Simon, you know the drill.'

'Sure, I keep it balanced by holding this wing until you get enough momentum.'

'Run beside her until we get too fast for you – the last thing I want is a wing to drop and hit the kerb. I've heard of planes landing on motorways but I think this is the first time a glider has taken off from a city road.'

From the front seat Charity saw the world about her emerging as dawn light diffused the sky. At the end of Hilliard Avenue she could see tiny points of red, amber and green following each other in succession, and it struck her as odd that traffic lights continued to operate in a city almost devoid of traffic. The lights reminded her that if the Blanik was not airborne by the time that Vic reached the end of the avenue, their black and white pillars would smash its wings off.

Paul settled in the rear seat and snapped on his harness. Turning to him Charity detected a surety of purpose and the emergence of a hidden talent. When they were together he sometimes gave the impression of vagueness but here was the man of action and it delighted her.

'I'll see you when all this is over,' Paul called to Simon who was holding the left wing tip shoulder high. 'Good luck.'

'Shalom,' replied the Israeli and Paul locked the canopy into position. He made a final check of the controls, raising and lowering the elevators and ailerons, then he passed Charity an electric torch.

'When you flash The Digger will know to start,' he said.

Charity pressed the switch and the Rolls Royce accelerated away. To her surprise the Blanik remained motionless. With sick fascination she watched the carefully coiled tow-line running out as the distance widened between car and aircraft. Suddenly there were no more coils, the line was taut and with a slight jerk the Blanik moved forward. Simon raced beside it but after a few seconds the speed increased and he had to let go.

Now it was the air rushing over the wings which kept the sailplane balanced on its wheel. Charity was aware that the Rolls was already approaching the traffic lights. Why wasn't the machine rising? Were the untested controls too stiff to fly it? Had a vital cable snapped?

The dual-control column angled back between her legs as Paul raised the elevators. Next second she felt as though she was in an express lift as the Blanik soared above the roadway until it was checked by the almost vertical tow-rope.

Paul leaned forward and pulled an orange-painted handle. The mechanism in the nose holding the tow-rope's ring opened, the nylon rope fell away and the Blanik was in free flight.

'So far so good,' Paul commented, trying not to betray the tension he felt.

'We aren't very high,' said Charity doubtfully, as roof-tops appeared to slide beneath their wings. 'Are we going to make it to Wembley?'

'If you look at the altimeter you'll see we're holding steady,' said Paul. 'The heat generated by a city causes the air to rise and I'm hoping it will be enough for us to at least maintain height.'

His right foot increased its pressure on the rudder pedal and he eased the control column sideways so the Blanik banked and then headed towards the column of smoke towering above the Wembley Football Stadium.

'See the instruments,' Paul told Charity. 'We're doing 50 knots and if you look at the Variometer you'll see that we are actually increasing our height at a rate of a metre per second.'

'I'll take your word for it,' said Charity. 'I've got work to do,' she added, adjusting her microphone.

Vic Kelly jammed on his brakes the moment he felt the tow-rope slacken. Climbing out of the car, he watched the graceful sailplane as it changed course before being obscured by roofs of distant buildings. He let the air whistle from his lungs in a deep-felt sigh of relief, then slowly walked round to the rear of the car to detach the tow rope. Halfway through the operation he had to lean against the boot.

'Jeez, but I'm Captain,' he muttered, rubbing his damp handkerchief across his forehead.

After a minute the feeling of sickness passed and he slumped wearily behind the wheel to drive back to where Simon Bernstein was waiting for him a mile up the avenue. The young man was jogging on the spot for warmth and looking anxiously over his shoulder as the sound of barking came closer. He saw a wave of dogs flow over a wall. In normal circumstances it would have been comical. Led by a large German Shepherd, the pack consisted of every size and breed of dog from a Doberman down to a Cairn terrier. What was not comical was their slavering mouths.

Spurred on by the scent of living prey, they surged across the roadway, no longer family pets but animals who had reverted to the primeval law of kill or die.

Simon sprinted towards the approaching car, but after a dozen steps sharp teeth crunched his heel and he sprawled headlong. Vic saw him fall and accelerated, his feeling of lethargy evaporating as he drove straight into the pack and had the satisfaction of feeling the wheels whump over several crazed animals. As the car stopped beside the snarling mound covering the young man he shouted, 'Quick, Simon!' But even as he yelled he knew it was too late – the leader of the pack had torn Simon's throat.

For a moment The Digger closed his eyes to blot out the horror, then the animals tried to get at him. Bloody muzzles smeared the windscreen and claws rasped the paintwork. He put down his foot. The car lunged forward, scattering the pack in all directions. But as The Digger drove away with his knuckles white on the wheel he dared not look in the rear vision mirror.

Paul banked the Blanik as they flew above the walls of Wembley Stadium, and Charity gazed down the wing at what had been the world's most famous football pitch. Now the long cremation trenches were infernos from which swirled clouds of greasy smoke. In areas once the preserve of cheering fans, hillocks of plastic-wrapped bodies waited to be bulldozed into the flames. It was not the sight of the plague's victims which brought tears to Charity's dark eyes but the thought that a short while ago Paul could have been cast alive into one of the open furnaces.

'Hold tight, here we go,' he cried and piloted the Blanik straight into the smoke. Immediately the light was blotted out and Charity felt the aircraft lift as though snatched by a giant hand. He pushed the column over hard so the Blanik wheeled in the tightest possible circle to remain within the ascending column. Charity clapped her hand to her mouth, and closed the ventilator with the other, as the stench of incinerating flesh filled the cockpit. Behind she could hear Paul gagging as he concentrated on riding the black thermal. Only the revolving hands of the altimeter indicated the speed with which they were borne upwards.

Their ears popped and after several minutes the density of the smoke thinned, though the super-heated air still lifted them at an astonishing rate. Several more minutes and they were clear of the smoke, and looking through the soot-grimed perspex Charity had the impression that far far below London was gradually turning beneath them.

'I've never known lift like it,' Paul declared. 'A lesser glider could not have stood it. If we go much higher we'll need oxygen so let's straighten out.'

He glanced at the compass, gently turned the Blanik in a north-westerly direction and adjusted the trim. Then, for the first time since their mad take-off, he relaxed as the sailplane flew effortlessly on a descending course. Charity slid open the ventilator and breathed deeply when cold air flowed in. As the effluvium receded she was reminded of Paul telling her on *Blue Flame* of the joys of motorless flight. The only sound was the hiss of air over the wings and she was awed by the immensity of clear sky arching above. Although the air-speed indicator showed they were travelling at 80 knots she had little sensation of movement except when a patch of vapour, seeking to become a cloud, appeared to whisk past them.

It was as though, having braved the fetor of the funeral fires, they had escaped from a world of violence and death into a calm and beautiful realm. The symbolism of it struck her so forcibly that she switched on the recorder so the inspiration of the moment could be held by tape for her future listeners. Paul listened to her words with a smile of approval as he kept his eye on the air-speed and rate of descent, fractionally moving the column from time to time in order to keep the compass bearing steady.

On his knee he had a motorist's map on which he had ruled a line from Wembley to Gayton. At that moment the sprawl of Watford was passing beneath them, Hemel Hempstead was five miles ahead and he could make out the silver thread representing the Grand Union Canal. In a few minutes he would be following the Fenny Pound where a century ago – or so it seemed – he and Charity had spent their first night together.

With an effort he returned to the job in hand, calculating on the margin of the map the distance to be travelled, their altitude and the rate of descent. As he reached the answer his lips tightened – unless he was lucky enough to find a thermal to lift them they would fall short of the target by over twelve miles. His temporary euphoria forgotten, he tried to slow their rate of descent but, despite every trick he knew, the Variometer needle continued to predict the failure of their mission.

16

Attention citizens of London. Attention citizens of London. By order of the Central Council of the New Britain Party, this radio station has been requisitioned in order that the objectives and routine commands of the Party shall be transmitted to you at regular intervals. At this moment the Party is taking control of the city to restore discipline necessary to overcome the present crisis. Before proclaiming the NBP Constitution and the emergency regulations it is with a sense of pride and privilege that I introduce your Leader . . .

It was the sound of an unknown voice which roused Vic Kelly from a fitful doze in his office. Despite antibiotics his head throbbed and the pain in his back caused him to groan. Panting heavily he sat upright on his white couch and gazed at the loudspeaker with reddened eyes as a new voice issued from it. It was a voice intended to give an impression of reassuring firmness, but an undertone of menace was allowed to emphasise key points.

'As Leader of the New Britain Party I appeal to my white fellow citizens to accept peacefully – indeed, gratefully – the new order which I and my party bring to this ravaged city,' it proclaimed. 'For years I, and my comrades-in-arms, have been planning for this day. For years we have stood in the wings, knowing that sooner or later we should be called upon to preserve what remains of our national heritage. For years we have watched increasing tragedy befall this nation. It began with cowardly politicians renouncing their imperial responsibilities. It was continued by those who wanted to dilute the blood of a once-proud people by waves of immigration. It was further compounded by a government whose aim is to see this country become a state in the East European mould.

'The men and women who support our cause feel pride in Britain's past and say "No!" to the alien ghettos successive governments have forced upon us, and they say "No!" to the secret Marxism of today's so-called leaders. As from this hour our movement will eradicate these evils and begin the mass repatriation of those who have brought this pestilence upon us . . . '

As the voice continued Vic hauled himself to his feet and staggered down the corridor to the studio. Through the glass partition he saw Phil Jason against the wall with his hands on his head. His chair was occupied by a fat man in NBP uniform who held a Luger pistol trained on the DJ's abdomen. A small transistor radio was held in his other hand.

'The Digger drew a deep breath and entered the studio.

'G'day, sport,' he said. 'You're coming on a bit strong, ain't yer?'

Lancelot Storm did not move a muscle.

'I was instructed to broadcast the Leader's message,' he replied, nodding to the cassette machine on Phil's desk. 'To this end I am prepared to lay down my life. Therefore it follows I shall have no compunction in shooting my hostage if you interfere with my orders.'

'I can see your point, sport,' said Vic reasonably, moving imperceptibly closer to the man with the gun. 'You know, I'm rather in your corner. Like you blokes say, this country has been going to the pack for years. Your pommy politicians should have kept to a white policy like Australia. I mean, it's heartbreaking to see the old homeland overrun by boongs . . . '

'Mr Kelly, do not think you can lull me into a false sense of security by sympathetic talk,' said Lancelot. 'Your attitudes are well known to us – the fact that your most popular programme is run by a black speaks for itself.'

'We have been misrepresented by the Zion-controlled media,' continued the voice from the transistor by which Lancelot could check that the tape was actually being transmitted. 'Many of you may have been led to regard the NBP as a group of cranks. We have been maligned as right-wing fascists in the fawning press, we have been ridiculed by the puppet broadcasting system, but let me tell you a great truth. There are many in high places sympathetic to our cause. There are comrades-in-arms in the services, there are men of vision in industry, all of whom . . . '

'Turn off that crap,' said The Digger. 'You can't take over London with a cassette. It came over the wire an hour ago that your leader has died of the plague.'

To his surprise the NBP man lowered his pistol and his shoulders shook.

'Then I am the last,' he said simply, 'but I have carried out my duty faithfully.' He turned and walked like a zombie from the room.

Phil Jason leapt back to his console and stabbed a button on the tape machine. He pulled a microphone close to his mouth and said, 'Well now, wasn't that a load of old codswallop?' in the same jolly tone he used before the days of the plague.

Through the partition came the muffled sound of a shot. The Digger shrugged and with one hand on the corridor wall returned to his office, stepping round the body of Lancelot Storm without a second glance. As he collapsed dying in his chair he wondered why the gunman had accepted his spur-of-the-moment story about the Leader's death . . . unless, of course, it was true.

The altimeter read 500 metres.

'We're going to have to land soon,' said Paul.

'Do you think we can reach Gayton with all those vigilantes on the loose?' said Charity.

'I've got an idea that might just work.'

His words were cut short by what sounded like a series of hammer blows. Glancing at the starboard wing they saw holes appearing as rifle bullets punched through the duralumin skin.

Paul pushed the stick forward to increase the speed and several minutes later he raised the brake flaps as the Blanik swooped down over the Fenny Stratford boatyard. The sailplane whistled low over rows of boats laid up for the winter and made a bumpy landing in a field beyond.

'All right?' he cried as they lurched to a halt and the port wing tip drooped to the turf.

'I'm fine,' said Charity. 'I take it we're going to go for a cruise.'

'That's right,' said Paul, swinging back the canopy. 'We'd better move fast in case those trigger-happy characters come looking for the Blanik.'

They climbed stiffly from the cockpit and waded through long grass to the towpath where *Blue Flame* was moored. While Charity cast off, Paul pulled out the choke and turned the ignition key, and after several attempts was rewarded by the vibrating note of the exhaust. With the black throttle handle pushed as far as it would go, the cruiser surged forward at double the legal speed limit of five miles an hour. Twin waves tumbled in its wake and washed over the banks.

While Paul held the spoked wheel and searched the landscape for signs of vigilante bands, Charity unlocked the cabin door and, after stowing the AP-13 canister and her tape recorder in a locker, set about making coffee.

'I think we can relax a little now,' said Paul as she handed him a mug. 'I noticed that the canal was blocked by an old narrowboat between Watford and Hemel Hempstead so our friends might not be looking for refugee boats further north.'

'I'm going to pretend you're right,' said Charity. 'I'm going to pretend that you and I are on holiday and the plague never happened.'

'That'll be rather hard,' said Paul, grimly.

She followed his glance and saw that a dozen distorted corpses were floating across the still green water ahead of them. Her hand rose to her mouth as the bows of *Blue Flame* disturbed them and a miasma of rotten flesh rose about them. Paul pointed to several suitcases and packs which lay scattered along the bank.

'Refugees,' he muttered. 'Looks like I could have been wrong about the lack of vigilante patrols up here.'

In the tense hours which followed the Freeman cruiser churned steadily along the canal, stopping only when Paul had to work it through the lock at the end of Fenny Pound. By mid-afternoon they reached the flight of locks which led to the Stoke Bruerne junction, once famous for its Waterways Museum. Now the tea-rooms which looked over the basin were boarded up and the sound of the engine reverberated hollowly from old warehouse walls. Paul remembered the last time he had cruised to Stoke Bruerne – then the locks had been jammed with pleasure craft and tourists swarmed on the quaysides.

'Not much further to go,' he said to Charity. 'Through the Blisworth Tunnel and we'll be nearly there.'

'I hope it's not too long for the sake of my claustrophobia.'

'Sorry, but it's Britain's longest navigable tunnel – over two thousand metres. And once we go in there's no turning back because it's only twelve feet wide. In the old days the narrowboats used "leggers" who lay on special boards and pushed them through with their feet against the walls. In fact, it's supposed to be haunted. Several men died in there a hundred years ago when a canal steamer called *The Wasp* ran into a narrowboat.'

'Thanks for that information. I think it could have waited until we reached the other side.'

After a few minutes of speeding between tree-lined banks Charity saw the black tunnel mouth set in the side of a wooded hill. Paul flicked a switch and the cruiser's searchlight probed the darkness. As the daylight faded behind them, the beat of the engine and the slap of the oily water against their bows echoed eerily. At intervals cascades of water streamed from air shafts set in the brick roof, drenching Paul and making Charity duck into the cabin.

'I hate this place,' she declared. 'And I wish you hadn't told me that story. How do the ghosts manifest themselves?'

'Oh, it's just a stupid tale,' said Paul. 'People are supposed to have heard cries in the darkness but there's nothing to be seen.'

'Then what's that?' Charity demanded, pointing through the windscreen to a vague white shape.

'Nothing supernatural. It's another boat.'

'Then why hasn't it got its lights burning? And its engine's not running.'

'Perhaps it just drifted in.'

As they approached the still craft Paul swung *Blue Flame* to port to edge past and Charity pushed it clear with a boathook.

'Oh God, Paul,' she cried. 'Look.'

As they slid past they saw two sprawled figures. One was the bloated body of a man half out of the cabin door as though he had died trying to reach fresh air. The other was of a girl sprawled against the edge of the cockpit. One arm hung down with its hand trailing in the water, and Paul saw the flesh of her fingers had been nibbled to the bones. He pressed the throttle lever down hard while Charity looked back sadly as the boat was again swallowed in darkness.

'They tried to escape only to die in here,' she whispered. 'Oh, Paul, that could so easily have been us.'

He nodded soberly.

'In the cupboard you'll find that bottle of rum you brought aboard,' he said. 'There's a little left. I think we could both use a shot.'

'Anything to get that ghastly taste out of my mouth,' she said.

Twenty minutes later, and better for the spirit which had combated the chill of the tunnel, Charity saw a small dot of light gradually expand into the tunnel mouth. Soon they were blinking in the outside air.

'That tunnel was the worst aspect of the whole trip,' she said with a shudder. 'I think in a previous life I must have died in a confined space. And I can't help thinking about that boat drifting in there.'

Paul turned off the ignition and steered *Blue Flame* to the bank. As it slowed he jumped on to the towpath and hammered two iron stakes into the ground to take the mooring lines.

'Gayton is over to the left,' he said. 'We just need to follow that lane a little way and we'll come to Poole Hall. It was a mock Gothic mansion given a new lease of life when the Bio-Synthetics people took it over. Pass me the canister, darling, and we'll be on our way.'

Charity locked the door of the cabin and, with Paul carrying the supply of AP-13 and her tape recorder, they followed the narrow road towards the tower rising above a spinney. The gargoyled gateway leading into the walled estate, as fantastical as the spires of the distant house, was guarded by two soldiers in a Landrover. As Paul and Charity approached one called, 'You wouldn't be Dr Mitchell by any chance?'

'Yes,' said Paul with a weary smile of triumph.

The other soldier spoke into a walkie-talkie.

'We've been on the lookout for you,' the driver said. 'Sir Robert had patrols sent out in all directions when word came that you'd managed to get out of London. Climb in. The old boy – I mean Sir Robert – is desperate to see you.'

A few minutes later the camouflaged vehicle skidded to a halt at the entrance to the hall. Sir Robert McAusland and several white-coated technicians were waiting on the steps.

'My dear boy,' he cried. 'Have you got the . . . '

'You'd better start processing it right away,' said Paul. 'There's only a fifty-fifty chance it's still animated.'

Sir Robert passed the container to his assistants who disappeared inside.

'You both look all-in,' he said with genuine concern in

his voice. 'Do you need food?'

'Later,' said Charity. 'First I want a bath and then I want a bed.'

'You do that while I go to the laboratory with Mac.'

'Oh no, you don't, Mitch. There's nothing more you can do now. Unless you get some rest you'll be a stretcher case again. I'll take you both to the room prepared for you.'

'Promise me that you'll let us know if the bacilli is still viable.'

'I promise you, laddie,' said Sir Robert, showing them into an old-fashioned bedroom. 'The bathroom is through there,' he added to Charity, while Paul collapsed on to the four-poster bed.

Twenty minutes later Sir Robert tapped on the bedroom door and came in. Beneath the canopy he saw that his friends had sunk into an exhausted sleep, Charity's golden brown arm thrown protectively over Paul's freckled chest. The old man felt strangely touched.

'I can no' wake you,' he muttered. 'My news can wait.'

'You are listening to Radio City and this is Phil Jason bringing you the good word at last. Here, on a special live link-up from Edinburgh, is the Prime Minister.'

'Good evening. It gives me immense satisfaction to announce that a special vaccine, known as AP-13, has been developed which will provide universal protection against the *Pasteurella pestis* virus which has literally decimated our country. Because of the vastness of the problem, and the fact that so many of our doctors and health workers have perished in the course of their duty, ordinary inoculation procedures are impossible. Therefore we developed AP-13 to be released into the air in the form of micro-droplets.

'You will receive immunisation by simply breathing the air in which AP-13 has been released, and I shall leave it to your local health officers to give you details of when the aerial dissemination will take place in your area. Let us all be thankful that the government's long-term plans, which were put into operation at the onset of the pestilence, have come to this successful fruition . . . '

The Prime Minister continued for another five minutes, neatly pointing out that the reconstruction would not only involve material rebuilding but also the planning of a more equitable and socially organised society – a society outside the old stream of political prejudice and spheres of military influence. He concluded by promising that as soon as life returned to a degree of normality the government would honour its pledge to hold a referendum on Britain's withdrawal from the Common Market . . .

Phil Jason said, 'And here in the studio is the GLC's Chief Medical Officer to give you the details of London's immunisation programme.' He pointed his finger at Peter Barnet who, hunched at a desk opposite him, began to read from a handwritten script.

'Tomorrow at noon Operation Airspray will begin,' he said. 'It will entail both military and commercial aircraft specially adapted to release tons of atomised AP-13 at low levels over the city. To get the best effect I would urge you to go to open spaces, such as parks, where helicopters will deliver the airborne vaccine in a highly concentrated form.'

When his message ended Phil Jason nodded his approval.

'There hasn't been much activity on the pop scene in the last few weeks,' he said into his microphone, 'but – as they used to say when I was a kid – you can't knock the rock, and this morning amazingly I was brought a tape from a new group called The Rainmakers. I predict when the charts are back with us it's going to zoom to number one. The song is 'Sweet Rain of Mercy', and I reckon it's so appropriate there must have been a leak.'

His hand travelled to the klaxon button on his desk.

'So folks, stay with Radio City for the good sounds, and here are the truly astonishing Rainmakers . . . '

Beep! Beep!

EPILOGUE

At the same time as the clouds of AP-13 microdroplets were settling over London, Hacker woke up in a cabin at the Misslou Motor Lodge on the outskirts of Natchez. The woman beside him was coughing terribly, and under the coverlet he felt fever heat radiating from her body.

'Oh honey, get me a doctor,' she gasped when the fit was over. 'I sure do feel so sick. It's like someone was turning a knife in my back.'

'Sure, sure, Marylee. I'll get you help,' he said, pulling on his jeans and sweat shirt.

'Please hurry, honey,' the girl pleaded as he reached the door.

'You just take it easy till I get back.'

He surreptitiously picked up his grip and within a minute he was swinging the apple-green Chevrolet on to the state highway. As the motel signs dwindled behind him, Hacker felt a familiar sense of isolation. Marylee was the second woman to take the plague from him since he had arrived off the tanker. He guessed now he was the only survivor of the plague pit, though the dead he had plundered had their revenge just the same. He was a carrier, immune to the infection himself but capable of passing it on to others.

If Marylee were alive when they found her she could give his description, and the highway patrols would be watching for him. He shuddered to think of the retribution which would follow his illegal entry and the introduction of plague to the New World. He could only go on until the money he had received from those gold coins ran out. His best bet would be to keep going north and try to make it into Canada. Beyond that the future was a frightening blank.

The road ran straight between moss-festooned oaks and

ahead a solitary figure stood beside a suitcase. As he drove past he saw it was a pretty teenaged girl in jeans and a tartan mackinaw. In the car mirror her dwindling image continued to wave. For a moment he hesitated, then slammed on the brakes and threw the car into reverse.

Picking up her suitcase the girl ran towards him.